A LOST KING

Also by RAYMOND DE CAPITE

THE COMING OF FABRIZZE

A LOST KING

By

RAYMOND DE CAPITE

DAVID McKAY COMPANY, INC.
New York

Library of Congress Catalogue Card Number: 61-12752

First edition

MANUFACTURED IN THE UNITED STATES OF AMERICA

VAN REES PRESS • NEW YORK

FOR

MARIE

A LOST KING

I

Once a long time ago my father told my mother that he thanked God for the gift of each day. Now it was different. Now in the mornings of that summer he complained about everything under the sun.

Our rooms and beds were separated by one wall and I would put my ear against it and listen to him with strange delight. Time and again he cried out that he was a prisoner of his ruined body, left with a son who was a prisoner of every fancy. He went on to curse his hot cell of a bedroom and the little dusty house that creaked and crumbled in the night like an old ship being tossed by the sea. He swept on like fire over the neighborhood and the city and the world. In the end he blamed me and God for everything.

I looked forward to hearing him first thing in the morning. I listened awhile and then got up to slice the oranges and put the coffeepot on the Grand stove. By then his deep rich voice was rising and falling. It was like a song to me.

"It's here and there and everywhere," he would be saying, from the bedroom. "I go to sleep with pain in my head and wake with pain in my back. The only excitement in my life is where it will get me tomorrow. And look how that smoke hangs in this room. It's like veils. I'll be smoked like a ham before it's done."

"You made a mistake when you bought this house," I said. "You should've tested the wind first. You'd have known right away it was better to live on the other side of the steel mills."

"Who the hell is that?" he said, in his bitter mocking way.

"It's your first mate, sir. I regret to report the crew's deserted. The men were going to mutiny, but they didn't want the ship. At the moment there's smoke fore and aft. And over and under. Let me know if you locate the bridge. And our course."

"Don't worry. Pretty soon we'll have a house under the smoke."

Sometimes it was hard for him to get out of bed. He would be lying there stiff and straight as though caught between frozen bedsheets. His angry brown eyes were fixed on some crack or wrinkle in the ceiling wallpaper. Pain was driven in deep like a knife between his shoulder blades and he couldn't even raise his arms. Curious things happened inside him during the night. Now and again he woke with an ache in his head from ear to ear.

"It's like a hot nail through my brain," he said. "It must be some kind of migraine."

"You need mineral oil," I said, teasing him.

"It's not in my stomach. It's in my head."

"Well, I was talking to Sam Ross. He thinks all this trouble comes from your stomach. And the way you feel about things is like more poison in your system."

"I'll need oil by the gallon. I'll be taking it from a pump."

Sometimes the pain closed around his knees.

"The bulldogs got me," he would say. "There's no end to this. A man climbs and climbs and then the rocks fall."

"You know what they say, Pa? There's no rose without thorns."

"Wait till you get old," he said. "You'll find out it's thorns and a dream about a rose."

For a time I was rubbing him at night with warm olive oil. When I rubbed his back he woke with pain in his legs. I rubbed his legs and the pain climbed into his back. There was one pain dancing around inside him or else he was loaded with them. One wintry night I rubbed him everywhere and he woke up with no pain at all. It was a miracle.

"How do I know I'm alive?" he said.

He was trying his legs and arms as though they were new. He risked a smile. The return of strength proved too much for him. There was nothing to do with it. He went out for a haircut and started an argument with the barber Regas. He left the shop in the middle of the haircut. He almost came to blows in a political discussion with the loungers in Lincoln Park. He gambled and lost and tore up a deck of cards in the Greek coffee house. He came lunging home to complain about my cooking and the dirt and disorder in the bedrooms. He gave me two weeks to find a decent job and quit for good the one I had on the watermelon wagon. It was so hard to be with him that I went out thinking it was pain that kept him human. Next morning he woke with that knife in his back again.

The first thing at those times was to turn him over and work the stiffness out of his arms and back. He was sharp and bony wherever I touched him. Often and on purpose I touched him before rubbing my hands together to warm them.

"Get away from me," he said. "You're like ice."

"I must have poor circulation of the blood," I said. "Maybe that's why it's so hard for me to work with my hands. And my feet are always cold, too. Walking tires me."

"Your head must be coldest of all."

"That's why I talk so much. Thinking hurts."

"It's your talk that hurts most."

It took so much time to help him into his dungarees that I made a suggestion. Seldom could I resist teasing him.

"Listen then," I said. "Why don't I fold up the bedsheet and pin it on you like a big diaper? You'll be all set for the day."

He drove his elbow into my side and knocked the breath out of me. Gasping and laughing, I sat down beside him on the bed. He got up and shuffled into the kitchen. He sat at the table.

He was working his arms when I came in to pour the coffee. I put four slices of white bread under the fire in the oven and when they were brown I turned them over. My father had taken two careful sips of coffee. Suddenly he was holding his breath as though he heard bugles in the morning. He went into the bathroom. After a while he came out with a challenging look to make clear that the function was pure delight for him and had nothing to do with need. He sat down and started to grind away on a slice of dry toast. For a moment we were gazing at each other in the pale early light.

"Your face is familiar," I said. "Very familiar. And there's something in your expression. The last time I saw an expression like that it was on the face of a man who bit deep into a rotten apple."

He stopped chewing.

"Haven't we met before?" I said, pinching him in the ribs.

"Goddam it," he said. "Don't do that."

"And I know that voice, too," I said. "I'm sure we've met somewhere. Let me think a minute. Wasn't it a bullfight in the south of Spain? Wasn't it you dancing there in the sunlight when that bull came down in a rush? What control you had! And then that bull caught you by the seat of your golden pants. Up you went. Up, up, up. You were spinning against the blue sky. And then you sailed past me and our eyes met. Both your hands went up, and I knew it was meant as a special kind of salute for me. And then you landed. You didn't move a muscle. What control you had!"

My father shook his head in bewilderment.

"Wasn't that you?" I said. "Wait then. Didn't I meet you on that coffee plantation in the jungles of Brazil? Now I remember you. You had a shining pistol and a white hat like a balloon. You had a whip forty feet long, and you were whipping forty natives at the same time. How could I forget a man who made a whip sing like that? Tell me something. It's between the two of us. How did you get out alive?"

"Where the hell did you come from?" he said.

"Let me introduce myself. Paul Christopher is the name. Here by special invitation. Look out the window, Pa. What a day it is! Look past the smoke. Look at that sun and sky. Something good is happening. I feel it in the air. Do you realize a baby's being born every five seconds or so? Right now in fact. While I'm saying this. But he's here! I hope he takes hold and never lets go!"

"He'll let go."

"Think of it, Pa. He's bringing something into the world that was never here before. Maybe it's a new hope or a new idea about things. Isn't it exciting? Wait, wait. His name is coming to me. It's Daniel. It's Daniel Carter! Ladies and gentlemen, I'm pleased to inform you that Daniel Carter has arrived with a grand idea. Hello, Daniel, hello! Now what's the idea?"

My father turned away.

After breakfast I made the beds and swept the bedrooms. I drew the torn window shades against the afternoon sun and then I went back to wash the breakfast cups and rinse out the gray enamel coffeepot that was shaped like a bell. My mother used to keep that pot warm and full for the friends who came to visit her all through the day. I broke up some bread and stepped out the back door to scatter it downhill for the brownish-gray little sparrows. In the spring the robins came, and once for a week there was a cardinal whistling sweetly to us.

We lived along the crest of a hill overlooking the industrial valley of Cleveland. Below was a sprawl of steel mills and oil refineries and chemical plants. Mill buildings were covered with reddish ore dust. The old brown Cuyahoga River twisted past them under the birdlike cranes that unloaded ore boats coming down from ports on Lake Superior. Railroad bridges were like opened black accordions over the river. Brown and yellow and orange boxcars curved away past fields of rusting scrap iron. Smoke was everywhere. I used to sit and watch it billow out of high strutting stacks. White flowers of it bloomed in the midst of orange veils. There were yellow plumes and then it blew dark and wild as storm clouds.

I went back into the house. My father was watching me. Those strong hands roped with veins were folded in his lap. He wanted me to shave him and yet he would say nothing about it.

I pinned the red and white dishcloth around his neck. I pinned it so tight that the muscles bulged below his ears.

"You out of your mind?" he said, ripping it off.

"Sorry, sorry."

I pinned the cloth again and gave him the brown razor

strap to hold. I stropped his fine straight razor and then I lathered him. I filled his ears with soap. He started swallowing and swallowing and cursing under his breath. His ears were slanted and so big it seemed he would hear if someone were drawing his wine in the cellar—which was the truth, if it came to that. I can vouch for it. His skin was red and leathery down to his bulging collarbone. Below it he was white and helpless somehow like a baby.

For a while I moved around humming and turning that straight razor in the palm of my hand. His face beneath a climbing tangle of sugary white hair was all bone and hollows and dissatisfaction. Those burning brown eyes watched me across the pirate nose.

"Are you finished dancing?" he said.

"I'm nervous this morning. Isn't it a little damp in here? My fingers are tightening. Really, Pa, I can't do my best work under these conditions. Do you want me to go ahead with this?"

"One more word and it's over. I'm warning you."

I started to shave him. It was good to touch him. It seemed I touched him only during a shave or massage.

"I'll be very careful," I said. "This must be perfect. I want you to look just right today."

"For what? For what?"

"A visitor is coming. What a thrill. My heart's pounding already. She was asking about you again. And again. And then again."

It was necessary to coax him into conversation. Talk made him feel better and so he set himself against it.

"Who was asking?" he said.

I leaned over to whisper in his ear.

"Sophie," I said, breathing hotly.

"Who?"

"Sophie Nowak. I can't get over the way she puts things. She goes right to the heart of it. 'How's your father?' she said. 'Is he still sleeping on the bed of nails?' "

"Tell her not to worry about my bed."

"Ten years ago yesterday she lost her husband."

"Lost him? My guess is she finished him off. She's got a face like a cauliflower."

"She wants to do things for us. She was telling me how she'd fix up this house. She'd plaster the cracks in the walls and then scrub everything down with a wire brush and pine soap. Including you and me. And then she'd put up lacy white curtains against the ugliness of the South Side. And then she'd toss garlands of Polish sausage here and there. She'll make *pierogi* for you. In the mornings you'll dance the polka together and in the evenings she'll knit winter woolies while you talk of world affairs. It'll be very gay and very satisfying for both of you. She gave me her word."

"Very pretty. We'll put on a show for the neighbors. It may be the last romance in the smoke here."

"Sophie said you're both in the same boat."

"And she wants to hold hands while we sink. Is that it?"

"She wants to know your favorite dish."

"Tell her it's privacy."

"I told her you like hot peppers and highly seasoned food. She winked when she heard it. And she pinched me when she said your name. She always does. Everything's all right until she says your name. And then she pinches me. I don't know what it means, Pa, but I walk a block out of my way for it. And there's something else. She offered to wash our clothes."

"She wants something in return."

"Well, she does want something."

"Who didn't know it?"

"She wants to brush and comb your hair in the evenings."

"If I lay my hands on her!" he cried.

"She said the same thing about you."

Right then I worked soap into his eyes with my forefinger.

"Get away!" he said. "That's enough of this!"

After shaving myself I went up to the corner delicatessen for him and bought the Cleveland *Plain Dealer* and a package of Model pipe tobacco. He was sitting in the Boston rocker on the porch when I came back.

"I'm not going out on the watermelon wagon," I said. "I'll go downtown and look for another job."

He was waiting to read the newspaper and smoke his pipe.

"Let's see if I have everything," I said. "A clean handkerchief and a comb. The key to the house. A map to find my way home if I get lost. Hope in my heart and iron in my bones."

"Didn't you forget something?"

"Name it."

"The harmonica."

"It's right here in my back pocket," I said. "I like music after lunch. And before it. And during it. It's good for the disposition. Try it some time. Listen then. Do you think I should wear a hat? It'll be hot and they say the afternoon sun is a danger to the brain."

"Have no fear," he said, with his dry laugh.

It was good to hear him laugh though it was usually at my expense.

"I'll bring you a surprise for supper," I said. "And something special for dessert. How about some walnuts or figs? How about a chocolate cake with custard in the middle?"

He said nothing.

"How would you like a new pipe?" I said. "How about one of those curved pipes? They curve out of sight down under your chin. Smoke curls up your nose and you forget where it's coming from. You can put yourself under a spell, Pa. You'll forget where you are."

"Buy the pipe."

"Really? Would you like it?"

"Do what you please," he said, turning away.

I was leaving early so that I could ride downtown in the bus with Peggy Haley. Halfway up the alley I turned back. I wanted to look at my father again. He was watching me.

"Good-by, Pa," I said, waving to him.

He turned away.

2

I remember the hushed voice and loving touch of my mother. Her name was Jenny. She would come softly in the dark of morning to sit on my bed and hold my hand. She would kiss my eyes and whisper some surprising thing in my ear. It was easy for me to pretend that I was still dreaming.

For a time I had this midnight cough. My mother would bring me hot wine with sugar in it and then she would rub my throat and chest with a clean burning salve. Dark beloved eyes came close to mine. Her breath was warm and sweet.

"I'll have to watch out for you," she said.

She whispered and kissed me as though hiding me in a safe secret place until morning. I used to cough and cough just to bring her to me. It was in the night that I realized she would never come to me again. All was lost but the dreaming.

I didn't stop that coughing right away. I went on with it and my sister Nina rubbed my chest for a few weeks. It was a different thing. Soon enough she tired of it.

"Make him stop that coughing," she said. "He's fooling around."

"Did you hear?" said my father.

He was drinking heavily in those days.

"I can't help it," I said. "I really can't."

To spite them I coughed and coughed. I was experimenting with harsh new coughs that tore at my throat. Sometimes they made me dizzy.

"Stop it!" said Nina. "I can't stand it!"

"You're breaking the rule," said my father. "My last warning."

"Rule? What rule?"

"I just made a rule against coughing in the house at night. I'm sick of it and so I made a rule against it."

"How can you do that?"

"Cough again and find out. Go ahead. Break the rule."

"I never heard of such a thing. It's impossible."

"Now I made another rule."

"What is it?"

"You just broke it," he said.

"But what was it?"

"The last rule is not another word out of you tonight! Not one!"

I went to bed and cried myself to sleep. My father was worse than medicine and I decided he had never been a boy at all. Surely he had been born old and tough like a tree to block my way and spoil everything.

Every day we were choosing up sides in the house. Nina and my father would be against me or I would be with Nina against my father. At times I was with my father against Nina. It was confusing. I would wake in the morning and try to remember whose side I was on. A bit of talk would change things around.

"Where's your sister?" my father would say.

"You mean Nina?" I said, stalling for time as usual.

"What a memory for names," he said. "A prodigy."

I was against him.

"Nina's washing her hair," I said.

"She left dishes and garbage in the sink."

"She needs a little time for herself, too."

"Do you think so?"

"I really do."

"Then you do the dishes," he said. "And be quick about it."

"It's not fair."

"It's fair to your sister. She needs time for herself. And it's fair to me. I want the dishes done."

"Maybe you should do them, Pa. That sounds fair to everybody."

"Maybe it is. But I'm stronger and smarter than you are. Now I'll give you fifteen minutes. And let that be a lesson to you."

"It's not fair at all!"

"What the hell are they teaching you in that school?

Are you in the fairy-tale class or what? Don't expect things to be fair. Get rid of that idea. It's another one of those bubbles. Don't be blowing them around here!"

It was so hard for Nina in the house that in the end she turned against both of us. She had to cook and clean and wash. She was only nineteen and like any girl she had other things on her mind. The truth is, she had the insurance man on her mind.

I have to admit she was a poor housekeeper. My father would come home from the steel mill and sit in the kitchen to smoke his pipe and drink glass after glass of his homemade red wine. At once Nina started sweeping the floor to impress him. She raised a cloud of dust.

"Stop, stop," he said. "I just had eight hours of this on the job. Don't you know enough to open a window or sprinkle the floor before you sweep? And why don't you cover the food? And what were you doing all day that you waited till now to sweep? I know, I know: you were waiting to sweep!"

Nina sewed up our clothes in such a way that the stitching looked worse than the hole. It seemed there were mice in our socks after she finished with them. She mixed things together in the Easy washing machine. All the colors shifted around. One day she forgot to take the pipe tobacco out of my father's dungarees before dropping them into that plunging machine.

"You forgot the pipe," he said.

Another time she was washing his favorite white broadcloth shirt. She washed it tenderly by hand and then rinsed it. Carefully she folded the buttons inside before sending it through the wringer. She hung it on the line in the back yard. She failed to put the clothespins in tight enough. A wind came up and blew that shirt down the hill where it got caught high in a sycamore tree. That evening I called my father outside to show it to him. I was excited. He stood and watched it flapping down there like a broken white bird. A muscle twitched in his jaw.

Something was wrong at every meal. Nina took no interest in cooking. Once for supper she served round steak and beans and potatoes and cabbage. Next two nights we had tomato soup. One day she was making a lamb stew and it burned at the bottom of the pot. She skimmed off the best of it and put it in another pot. She forgot it and half an hour later it burned again. She changed it to another pot. The stew left for supper had this dead black look and taste.

"What the hell's going on?" said my father. "Is this what's left of a pound and a half of spring lamb? It's like magic. Black magic, too, from the way it looks. And it wasn't enough for you to ruin the lamb. I see you put in carrots and green peppers and potatoes. Why did you stop there? Why didn't you put in the salad and bread and coffee? It would've been a complete triumph in one pot!"

Nina was ready to cry.

"But I ate a big dish of that stew," I said.

"Is that so?" he said, wheeling on me.

"I was hungry when I came from school. I ate my share of it. I'll just have some salad for supper."

"Did you like the stew?"

"It was all right, Pa."

"You can have this, too," he said. "You can have my share. And I'll sit here while you eat it. All of it."

"It's not his fault," said Nina.

"I wasn't talking to you," he said. "He climbed on the horse and we'll let him ride. . . . How's the stew?"

"It's good," I said.

"Be careful," he said, ominously.

I took a deep breath.

"This stew is a treat," I said.

He swept the dish off the table.

"Clean it up and go to bed!" he said. "Right now!"

Later that night two fellow workers from the steel mill came to visit him. He was in such a drunken fury that he turned the oven on full blast to get rid of them. Those two men sat there sweating in the kitchen. They couldn't stand it. Suddenly they leaped to their feet. They were dancing round as though the floor itself had gone hot. They were gasping and grabbing for their coats and plunging through the door. My father burst into laughter.

After a bad day in his crane at the mill he rushed home to complain about everything in sight. He tasted the beef soup and then jumped with a cry and threw dish and all against the wall. He always threw it against the same spot over the sink. Nina burst into tears and ran into her bedroom. I sat there eating while my father cursed and pounded the table. Dishes and cups were dancing.

"Do you call this living?" he said. "Work and sweat like an animal and then come home to this? Dishwater for supper!

You should be ashamed of yourself! I say there's no love in you! You won't even take the time to cook a decent meal for your own flesh and blood! You couldn't hold a dog in the house with this food! By Christ, he'd rip your apron off! Why the hell do you even wear an apron?"

Nina was crying.

"Look around," he said. "Look at this house. Five rooms to clean and it's like a tornado hit! What the hell do you do all day? I know, I know: you brush your hair and paint your lips and look in the mirrors. I wish I had a dollar for every time you saw yourself. You should have a twin sister. You could spend the day holding hands and looking at each other!—What're *you* doing?"

I was eating. I was eating everything in front of me. I finished my soup and snatched his bread. I speared some boiled beef. I was reaching for the lettuce and tomato salad when he turned on me.

"Eating," I said.

"I hear it," he said, grinding his teeth. "How was the soup?"

"It was all right."

"Is that the truth?" he said, looming in a dangerous way.

"It wasn't so bad."

"I'll give you one more chance."

Nina was sobbing.

"It was remarkable," I said, bracing myself.

I jumped sideways as he turned the table over.

"Get out of my sight," he said, softly. "Quick, quick. I don't want to see your face tonight."

Hour after hour he sat in the kitchen. I watched him through my bedroom door. He was drinking wine. His big brown work shoes sat on the floor beside him. They were like puppies. There were dark stains of sweat under the arms of his dungaree shirt. Now he was looking at his black cap and lunchpail on the cupboard. Beside them were his work gloves like smashed swollen hands. His glance went up to his black hat on top of the gleaming new refrigerator. It was the hat he saved for special occasions and for remembering. He got up and put it on. He sat down again. He was leaning forward in the chair. Surely he was thinking of my mother. Long into the night they would stay up to hold hands and drink wine and laugh. Her laughter was hushed and sweet. He would snort. Remembering, I got out of bed just to let him know I was there with him. He watched me. He beckoned.

"What's the matter?" he said.

"I can't sleep. I guess I'm thirsty."

He gave me half a glass of wine.

"It's good," I said.

"I know. For you everything is good. For me everything is bad. It's a little difference of opinion we have."

"But it really is good."

His hatbrim slanted down in a kind of thin black salute.

"You may be right and right about things," he said. "But in the end you're wrong. I may be wrong and wrong but in the end I'll be the one that's right."

"Is there enough wine for you?"

"I need an ocean. This is the last barrel."

"We'll make more. You'll have it all winter."

"We'll see. Go to bed. Sleep here and not in school."

In the morning it was the same old story with him. Before dawn he would be moving here and there as though searching in every corner of a strange house. Presently he slipped into our rooms to tear the bedcovers off us. His eyes were wild at the emptiness of the day.

"Get up, get up," he said. "Are you on vacation?"

It happened every morning. He came like a thief into our rooms to whip the covers off. It was bad for me and worse for Nina. It was a shock and a shame to her. I used to wake up angry. I followed him around and glared at him.

"Do you know what happens to boys who look like that?" he said.

"Like what?"

"Like you're looking at me."

"What happens to them?"

"They see a star."

"A star?"

He smacked me on the back of the head.

"What about it?" he said. "Did you see it?"

"I guess so."

One morning I woke before he did. I dressed and put the mop in my bed and covered it. He slipped in and ripped the covers off. His mouth fell open. I scooted past him to escape a sweeping backhand. It was like being on the offensive. It made me reckless. A while later I complained about the coffee. I knew he made it. He had no consideration for us. He boiled coffee grounds right in the water and then killed the taste of it by putting whiskey in his cup. That coffee was black as night and seemed to be dissolving my teeth. There was always a layer of grounds in cups so stained they needed scouring.

"What is this?" I said, sipping the coffee.

"What?" said Nina. "What's the matter, Paul?"

"Shame on you," I said. "Your own flesh and blood."

"What are you talking about?"

"This coffee. Why, it's like a poison. Really, Nina, it's very cruel of you to do these things to us. I mean it."

"Do you?" said my father.

"I really do."

He hit me on the back of the head and took my cup away.

"Now tell me how you feel?"

I saw a star and felt resentment.

All that day I had a big thirst for revenge. I rushed home from school. No one was there. I was kicking chairs and slamming dishes around when there came a soft rapping on the door. A bearded old man seemed to be talking to me even before I opened the door.

"What's the meaning of this?" he said, in a low singing voice.

"The meaning of what?"

"Where is everybody?"

"Well, my father's working. My sister must be shopping."

"It's your father I came to see, my boy."

"He'll be home in an hour or so. He's working."

"Say no more. I'll wait for him. It's an old promise. Ashtabula, Ashtabula. I wonder if I might trouble you for a bite to eat while I wait for him. My name is Lance. Lance Caulfield."

I was bewildered. I was gazing at the white hair swirling round his ears and billowing down into the luscious beard. That beard was like a handful of summer cloud. Hidden sapphire eyes watched me. His graying shirt was open at the collar where a silver crucifix gleamed within the snowy whirls of his beard and chest hair. He wore a buttonless brown overcoat that looked as if it had been chewed up by a dog.

"And your mother?" he was saying, as he closed the door.

"My mother passed away."

"I'm sorry, my boy."

"Eggs," I said. "How about some eggs?"

"Perfect, perfect. Three will do."

He sat down at the table. I made coffee. I fried three eggs in butter and toasted four slices of bread. I put everything in front of him at the same time so that I could sit and watch him. I wanted to hear that rich singing voice again.

"My own dear mother came from Ireland," he said. "One winter there she and my grandmother and grandfather ate thirty bushels of potatoes. The next winter they ate forty bushels of potatoes. And the next winter fifty bushels."

"And then?"

"She came to try her luck in America. She met and married my father. He was an artist. A painter. He painted pictures of her. All day. My mother could never understand why he wanted pictures of her when she was there in the flesh. She began to think there was more to be said for potatoes."

"Really?"

"Probably. Now look at me. But you mustn't look too close. I have my father's temperament, my boy, but no talent. A talent only for living. Would you believe I was once regarded as a dashing figure? And then I found myself dashing to catch buses. And dashing to the bank. And dashing to pay grocery bills."

He finished the eggs and cleaned the dish with his bread. He sipped coffee and wiped the beard away from his mouth with his forefinger. His eyes were roving. They fell on my father's pipe and hat on the refrigerator. He got up.

"A pipeful would be excellent," he said. "Do you mind?"

"Not at all."

He filled the pipe and lit it. Puffing, he studied the hat. Gently he took it down and turned it in his smooth white hands. My father would have liked the way he touched it.

"Beautiful," he said, sitting down. "How soft it is. And the color is perfect. It's a living black. Like the night."

He put it on. That black hat was perfect above swirling hair and clear startling eyes. I watched him. He gazed at me and then beckoned. I went to him. He wanted me to stroke his beard.

"Are you thinking deep thoughts?" he said. "You should always ponder and meditate when you stroke a beard. Wait then, wait then. Give me your other hand. Put it on my heart. Do you feel it beating? Alone in the dark and so brave. Yours is the same. Yours is the same. Keep stroking the beard. Think and feel. The heart sings alone like a bird. Think and feel, my boy."

Sweet smoke from the pipe engulfed me.

Lance Caulfield was putting my hands together as though for prayer. He was whispering as he turned me to send me back to my chair.

"Promise me," he said. "Promise me one thing."

"Anything."

"Promise to tell your father that Lance will return. I kept my promise. I kept mine, I kept mine. Ashtabula, Ashtabula."

He went away.

All at once my father came lunging through the door. It was such a shock to me that I burst into tears. After a while I remembered what happened. I tried to explain it to him.

"Lance will return," I said, finally. "Ashtabula, Ashtabula."

My father was looking at the top of the refrigerator where his pipe and hat had been. His dark eyes burned shut and seemed to leave his face in ashes. He put his hands in his pockets and went into the bedroom. He closed the door, softly.

First thing in the morning he hit me twice. Little by little I could feel my head going numb. It was happening more quickly all the time. My father hit me so often in those days that the neighbors explained everything about me by saying I was stunned. I still have this feeling he slapped something out of me, or into me.

After hitting me he ordered me to go down the cellar and fire the furnace. Before going down those creaking stairs I dropped a scrub pail to scatter the mice. That pail banging down the stairs brought a scream from Nina and a wild cry from my father. They thought I fell. My father rushed over.

"What happened?"

"I dropped the pail to scare the mice away."

"When will you learn to think before you act?" he said. "When will it be, when will it be?"

He smacked me.

I went downstairs crying. I put newspaper and sticks in to start the fire. I decided to cut school and go downtown. To spite him further I threw one of his winter boots on the fire before putting in the coal. I was on my way downtown when the smell of it filled the house.

That night he gave me a terrible beating. Next morning I threw in the other boot and went downtown again. He gave me another beating. All in all it was worth it.

3

After a time it was so good to be with Nina that my father became suspicious. No longer did she complain about work in the house. Each day she managed to get the cleaning and shopping done. She sang songs while ruining our food and she was blushing and trembling in every corner. The house came alive with stirring sounds. All around us were delicious little sighs and soft moans of delight and sudden bells of innocent laughter. Once I heard her whispering hotly in the clothes closet. I flung open the door. She flung her arms around me.

"I forgive you for everything!" she cried. "Now and forever!"

Life was so sweet for her that one night she danced around the kitchen with the broom and then the mop. My father sat there watching with wild steady eyes and head cocked as though listening for the footfall of the enemy. The very next night Nina danced out of our lives with the insurance man Andy Bobbio. My father was left watching me. He broke mop and broom over his knee and then locked the door against Nina.

"Didn't I tell you to watch them in the day?" he said. "What the hell were you doing here?"

"I was watching," I said.

"You watched them go out the door! Everything was happening and you saw nothing! Next time I'll tell you to watch the sky! Why didn't you tell me what was going on? Why didn't you warn me?"

"You were at work."

"And so everything happened tonight? Is that it? They met and ran away to get married."

I said nothing.

"I'm talking to you," he said. "What were you doing?"

"I was thinking."

"I know, I know," he said. "You were thinking if you had a camera you'd take their picture."

"And then I said a prayer."

"A what?"

"A prayer for Nina to be happy."

"Good for you! Millions of people are in misery all over the world and God is going to make Nina happy! Do you want to pray? Pray for your wits. Pray for strength. Pray for luck. You'll find out what it is without a sister. Go back to bed!"

He stayed up all night. He was raving. Nina had baked a farewell sponge cake as a gift and he threw it out the window. Some of it stuck to his hands.

"It's like cement," he said. "It's made with the left hand like everything else for us. Let her cook for him now. Now it's his turn. By Christ, I think they deserve each other. They look for love and find justice! It's the same old kick in the ass!"

All along I had been watching Nina and Andy. Warmth of feeling spilled over between them and yet I had no idea they were planning to elope. Day after day he kept turning up for coffee and talk. I was on the alert. Nina made weak coffee and her talk was even weaker.

"Look who's here," Andy would say.

He swept off his porkpie hat and his curly hair jumped up.

"Stop, look, and listen," he said.

His hair was like black broccoli.

"Never fear, Andy's here," he said.

There was no doubt about it. He was a feast for the eyes in that smoke on the South Side. He had a dimpled baby face with eyes dark as his hair. He was wearing a gray flannel suit and a black and gold bowtie like a rare butterfly. Round his waist was a black shoestring belt with a silver buckle. He wore black moccasins with pretty leather bows. Nina and I were goggling at him.

"Don't be greedy," he said. "Save part of me for later."

He reached into his pocket for a cigarette case. He held it to catch the light and blind us. A moment later he was lighting a cigarette and watching Nina through the smoke. He was watching her in a way that forced me to look at her. Just about then he crossed his legs to show us gray socks with pink rabbits dancing on them. There was no place to go from the socks and so Nina and I went back to start with his hair again. So dazzling was he that a boy named Danny Poulos used to throw stones at him in the alley.

"You think this is something?" said Andy. "You should see my underwear. My underwear, that's right. You'd applaud."

"Really?" I said.

"You've had enough excitement for one day," he said. "And another thing. I forgot the plums."

"Plums?"

"I always carry plums in my pocket. When I see someone with his mouth open like that I always put a plum in. A plum, that's right. You heard me. Your ears don't flap over."

He sat there sipping coffee and smoking cigarettes. Nina whirled around him with mop and broom and pail. Never had she worked so hard. The house was in fair order while Andy made those visits.

"Don't lift that couch," he'd say, jumping up to help. "Listen, Nina, you should be more careful. You'll strain yourself doing things like that. What's the matter with Paul? You work like a slave here. A slave, that's right."

My teacher Miss Riordan used to say that when a man called you a slave he had a change of masters in mind.

"When do you rest around here?" said Andy. "Why are

you on your feet all the time? Sit down a while. Who's driving you? I don't like this. For one thing you'll ruin your legs. Your legs, that's right."

Nina blushed. She looked beautiful to me with her black hair and those brown eyes flecked with gold. It seemed I was seeing her for the first time.

"What do you do?" said Andy, turning to me.

"I just started high school. Lincoln High."

"He was set back twice in school," said Nina.

"Don't worry about it," said Andy.

"That's why they set me back," I said.

"How about the important things?"

"What important things?"

"Can you make change for a dollar?" he said. "Do you feel in your heart there's happiness right around the corner? Are you willing to sacrifice yourself for the good of the team?"

"What team?"

"Are you a good athlete? Can you fly a kite? What if I bring a kite? Will you go out and fly it?"

"Save your money."

"Hold still then. I'll carve your statue in this butter."

"Can you do it?"

"I wish I had a plum."

He turned to Nina.

"Just look at your hands," he said. "Look how red and raw they are. They'll look like liver in another month. Liver, that's right. You should wear rubber gloves if you put them in water so much. All the girls do. Don't you know that?"

Nina was looking at her hands. She was on the verge of tears.

"It's incredible and unbelievable," he said. "Don't you realize you're like a prisoner in this house? Don't you ever get out for a good time? Do you like music? How about it?"

"Oh, Andy," she said.

"Do you ever go dancing? Do they ever take you out to dinner or a show? Let's start at the beginning. Now I want you to think hard. Did anyone here ever say thank you for anything?"

"Oh, Andy."

"Now I need plums for both of you," he said. "I didn't know I was delivering the news. Believe me, Nina, this is an old story. They take you for granted here. They don't appreciate you at all. Tomorrow will be just like today. But you'll be a day older and more worn out. It's all the same to them as long as the house is clean and their supper's on the table. I've seen it like this. My work takes me into a lot of houses. Consider your father. I don't want to say anything against him. But he's like an animal. An animal, that's right."

Andy thought he better bring me into it.

"Isn't that right, Paul?"

"What's that?"

"Tell the truth now," he said. "Doesn't your father act like an animal around this house? Doesn't he?"

Andy touched his bowtie and then gave me another look at the rabbits on the socks. The dancing rabbits did it. I was with him.

"An animal?" he was saying.

"He really is," I said.

Right then my father came in. He slammed his lunch-pail and gloves down on the cupboard. He looked at no one. His black cap curved down on both sides from its peak and seemed to be cupping his face until the big bones bulged.

"Good afternoon," said Andy. "I'd like to talk to you."

My father wheeled on him with that crazed look.

"Now's your chance," he said.

"Well, Mr. Christopher, maybe we should talk about insurance."

"Insurance?"

"Insurance against things happening."

"There's no insurance against things happening."

"I mean it's good to have insurance in case things happen."

"You mean it's good for those who collect on the insurance."

"Well, Mr. Christopher, I wouldn't put it in that way."

"You wouldn't put it in any way at all. You're sitting in my kitchen and drinking my coffee. And you're telling me I'm going to die. This is important. This should be cut in stone. But all I hear from you is things will happen. It's wind through the leaves. And then you say insurance is a good thing for me and what you mean is hard cash for somebody else. What you want me to do is pay my way out and leave something behind."

"Maybe I better be going," said Andy.

"Now you're talking," said my father.

At night Andy waited for Nina around the corner in Lincoln Park. In the day he kept turning up at the house when my father was at work. He brought gifts. He brought pies and cream puffs for Nina. He brought Hershey bars for me. I sat in that kitchen watching them and eating pie and candy until I broke out with boils on my neck.

By now they were touching each other in a delicate way as though touching harps. Once he dared put his hand right over hers while she was pouring coffee for him. So thrilling was it that she poured the coffee in his lap. She burst into tears. He said it didn't matter. He didn't mind having hot coffee in his lap as long as she made and poured it. She laughed through her tears.

After a few weeks they didn't talk much at all. Andy gazed out the window. Nina sat with her hands folded in her lap. I could hear them breathing. It seemed they were blowing up invisible balloons. Even when they talked I couldn't understand it.

"I was thinking," he would say.

"I know," she said, blushing. "So was I."

"I was sort of wondering here," he said.

"Say it," she said.

"But there's Paul," he said.

"What is it, Andy?" I said, through a mouthful of peach pie.

"Say it," she said.

"But Paul," he said.

"Yes, Andy?" I said.

"Say it then," she said, urgently. "Please."

"I wish I could," he said, breathlessly pale.

"Never mind," she said. "I think you did."

"Did he?" I said.

Three days later it was over for my father and me. Andy came through the door. Nina hurried to him with the mop. They stood beside the refrigerator. They were watching each other as though for a false move. I held my breath. They had caught me up in it.

Andy didn't know what to do and so he swept off his hat. His curly black hair jumped in a coil. Nina sighed. Andy was swallowing so hard that his bowtie fluttered. They came together in a kiss. The mop fell to the floor. Nina was clinging helplessly and they swayed there in the gold slanting haze of sunlight. I turned away in a kind of shame. For some reason my heart swelled with pity for my father.

They eloped on that very night. My father was working the afternoon to midnight shift in the mill. Nina came to me in the bedroom before going away. She sat on the bed and took my hand.

"Paul," she said. "Are you awake, Paul?"

"Yes."

"Can you hear me, honey?"

"Yes."

"Listen to me, Paul. I won't be seeing you for a few days. It's just a few days. I'm going to marry Andy."

"All right."

"Are you really awake? Do you understand what I'm saying?"

"I guess so."

"Look at this. Andy brought you something."

"I don't want any candy."

"He brought you something else."

"What is it?"

"He brought you a harmonica."

I took it. The gold of it was warm and moist from her hands.

"Tell him thanks."

"You can play songs, Paul. You can play songs for everybody."

"I guess so."

"And you can play a song for me when I come home. I'll be here on the weekends to clean the house. Is it all right, Paul? Say it's all right. I love Andy and I have to be with him. Can you understand?"

"Yes."

She was beautiful. Her black shining hair held the light and her dark eyes were big and soft with tears. She touched my face and I thought of my mother. Suddenly I realized how much I loved Nina. Now it would never be the same with us. She belonged to Andy. I remembered that kiss and I hated him.

"I feel so bad inside," she was saying. "So bad."

"Why should you?"

"It's like I'm doing a wrong thing. I shouldn't be leaving now. I shouldn't be leaving you and Pa alone here."

"We'll be all right. I'll take care of things."

"Oh, Paul, I love you so. It just seems like you realize things too late. And I love Pa, too, with all his ways. Why can't things ever be perfect? Why is life so hard all the time?"

"Don't go crying."

"I was thinking about Ma, too. I was wondering what she'd say if she knew I was leaving like this. It's a selfish thing, Paul. I feel ashamed of myself."

"Don't talk like that."

"I think Pa's right. There's a worm in the fruit. Wouldn't it be awful if he's right about everything?"

"I think he's wrong. I really do."

"I'll pray for us. I'll pray with all my heart. And I'll be here on the weekends to help out. You'll see. Tell Pa."

"You know what?"

"What?"

"I wish I could play this harmonica right now. I'd play a song for you. Just for you to be happy, Nina."

"Oh, Paul."

Tearfully, we hugged and kissed each other.

Just about then Andy was down in the cellar stealing a quart of wine. He failed to closed the spigot tight and the rest of that last barrel dripped away in the night while my father was raving.

My father never forgave him. Sometimes I went down the cellar and found him gazing at the old bloodlike stain in the cracked cement of that floor.

4

A girl may not know how to prepare a meal or sew on a button or sing a song to give hope for the day. It means nothing. It is good to have her in the house even if she sits for hours in front of a mirror brushing her hair and looking into her own eyes.

Disorder came when Nina went. Cups and dishes filled the sink. Dust gathered on furniture and floors. Towels and bedsheets and curtains turned gray as the sparrows. The windows went blind with soot.

"What the hell's the difference?" said my father. "There's no reason to look out or in."

We kept forgetting things. We forgot to change our clothes. Now and again he would be watching me across the table as though picking up a strange new scent. He would go out to buy coffee and forget sugar for the coffee. I bought meat and forgot bread. For a time we forgot that we were human beings.

"Who goes there?" he'd say, at supper. "What disguise is that? Look at your hair. You need a haircut. And look at the collar of your shirt. Don't you ever wash your neck? When did you take a bath last? You're beginning to smell like a third cousin. No wonder I get notes and notes from that school."

"School?" I said, paying little attention to him. I had learned to eat as much as possible before the dishes started to fly.

"School, yes, school. It's that yellow building on Scranton Avenue where you go to keep warm in the day. Did you lose your way again? Wait then. What about the list of things I made out for you? Did you change the beds? Did you wash the underclothes? Did you buy coffee and bread? Did you pay the electric bill? Did you put cheese out for the mice? Look at me when I talk! You're like a wolf at the table! One of these days you'll drown in the soup!"

It was better for me when he operated the fast-plant crane that unloaded ore boats in the steel mill. That work exhausted him. But his age and the stiffness in his back forced him out of the crane. The dock superintendent kept him on as a kind of janitor and watchman in the locker room. Every day after sweeping up he sat watching coats and hats and cats and the weather. The only break in that routine came when he was called on to help replace broken cables in the cranes. My father took no pride in being a watchman. He had to blame someone for wasted days and so he blamed me.

He gave me bad beatings. Night after night I went to bed with my body aching and my head feeling dead as a tin can from his slaps. When I stayed out of range he threw his slippers at me. He was quick as a cat. He had his slipper off and flying at me before I could move.

"Let's see if I got things right," he said. "I told you to put cheese in traps for the mice. Now you were nervous after what happened with the electric bill. You took half a pound of Swiss cheese down the cellar. You forgot the knife to cut the cheese and so you came back upstairs. You forgot the cheese. And that was the end of it. Why didn't you put knives and forks and napkins for the mice? Do it next time. They'll be back. And what about this?"

He hit me on the forehead with a slipper.

"Wait, wait," he said. "Don't go away yet. Let's talk about the electric bill. Now I gave you five dollars to pay that bill. You were on your way to the bank during the lunch hour at school. The next thing you knew you were in Lincoln Park playing the harmonica for the bums who sit there all day. A man called Lefty did an Irish jig. You enjoyed it. The next thing you knew you were across the street in Wheeler's Bar setting up drinks for them. One of them drank a toast to me. Was it Lefty? Have I got it right? And then you forgot about school. And the next thing you knew you had a dollar left."

He hit me on the side of the head with the other slipper.

The next thing for me was work in that house. Soon I was doing the cleaning and shopping and cooking. For three months Nina came to help us on the weekends. My father threw her and Andy out the first time. He made a speech declaring his independence.

"I don't need help from him or anyone," he said. "He robs the bank and throws me a few nickels. It'll never be! From now on I ask for nothing and give nothing! It's finished!"

As the house fell more and more into disorder he made another speech. He pointed out that Nina was his flesh and blood. Andy was still barred. My father was sensible enough under the uproar.

By the end of the third month, however, Nina let it be known she was neglecting her own house to help us. I knew the tide was turning when she insisted I watch close and learn how to prepare food and change beds and run the Easy washing machine. Soon she was coming every other weekend and then she started to turn up in the middle of the week when there was nothing to do but argue. She explained that she was being forced to make a decision between her husband and us. I didn't know who was forcing that decision but I knew which way it was going. Down went my father and I. Nina announced that she could not save everybody and so she had to save herself to save Andy. My father said that neither she nor insurance nor God could save Andy. There was a celebration of the disaster. Nina said something about her right to have the oak-leaf pattern dishes and cups of my mother as a sort of dowry for Andy.

A shower of leaves was to follow. My father embraced the cupboard. It was too heavy and for an instant he was dancing in a fury down below it. Finally he tipped it forward and it smashed down on the floor. The house shook and plaster crumbled in all the walls. Nina burst into tears and ran out.

"They want everything!" cried my father. "They'll strip me to the bone! It's a good thing my clothes don't fit him! By Christ, I should have my head examined for raising children! I swear it's better to raise hogs and cattle! At least I can fatten them up and have meat for the winter!"

I was sitting there and so he turned on me.

"What's holding you?" he said. "Get your things and get out! That door leads both ways!"

I sat and thought about it. He went on raving. There was no place for me to go. Besides, I belonged with him.

Before and after school I did my best to keep the house in order. Each day I swept the floors and dusted the furniture. On the weekend I changed the towels and bedsheets and then I mopped every room. Cooking supper for him was easy. It turned out that the food was all right if he could taste hot pepper.

"I need some fire in my life," he said.

I loaded the food with black and red pepper and hot sauces like Tabasco. Sometimes I went too far with it. He would sit there with mouth and lips aflame. Beads of sweat the size of pennies popped out on his forehead.

"This food's too hot," I said. "I finish eating here and it's like a hot coal inside me all night."

"A hot coal is what you need inside you. It's what's missing."

"But I can't even taste the pork chop."

"Don't eat then."

"But I'm the one who cooked it. Don't you know you wake me every night with your cries? We'll be all ashes inside."

"Then it's ashes in and out."

I took out the harmonica and tapped it.

"Now what?" he said.

"I think I'll practice awhile."

"Good, good."

"Would you really like to hear it?"

"Why not?" he said. "What a surprise! It's like Santa Claus down the chimney! Can you really make music out of this misery?"

"I'll try," I said, without thinking.

His dark eyes closed. The bones in his face bulged.

"Listen to me a minute," he said, softly. "At your age I was working in a coal mine in Pennsylvania. Do you know that? You seem to be going backward. Now it's the harmonica. In a couple of years I'll be tickling your toes and warming a bottle for you. Get out. I'll clean the kitchen myself."

Out I went. I strolled up to the Greek coffee house around the corner. I sat in the doorway and played the harmonica until the owner Theodore Ampazis called me inside. I played a few songs for him and the card players. He gave me a bottle of ginger ale and a piece of *baclava,* a pastry made with honey and nuts. Theodore had such a gentle way with me that I stopped to see him in the mornings on my way to Lincoln High School.

"I smell whiskey," he said, one morning. "Do you drink, Paul?"

"My father lets me put some whiskey in my coffee. He says it wakes me up and takes the chill out of me."

"Play a song or two while I mop up."

I played for him. I played until I forgot about school.

"That's enough," he said. "You better be going. Don't forget your coat. And your lunch."

I went to school by way of Lincoln Park. I had packed a ham sandwich for Lefty Riley. Lefty was a retired lake sailor. He used to sit and wait for me in the mornings. Never did he fail to stand up and shake my hand. I looked forward to it.

"How's your father today?" he said.

"About the same, Lefty."

"I was thinking about him. And about that ax you mentioned. The ax his father gave him when he left Italy."

"What about the ax?"

"An oak log," he said, smiling. "What you ought to do is order an oak log for him every day. Early in the morning he'll go down the cellar and chop hell out of that log. He'll get everything out of his system. He'll be at peace the rest of the day."

"It's a good idea."

"Thanks for the sandwich, Paul. Get going. I think you're late again. I'll bet you got a cherry pepper in the lunch."

Lefty was right. I had a cherry pepper. I was always the center of attention when I opened my lunch in the school cafeteria. I would show off by eating that hot pepper with no bread to ease the sting of it. My friends were delighted by this performance. I did it for love of Peggy Haley who lived in the house at the corner of the alley. Peggy had black hair and pale blue eyes. She was plump and beautiful.

"Is Paul going to do it again?" said Sally Walters.

"He's just about ready," said Joe Faflik.

"I think he's silly," said Peggy.

I held the red pepper up like a magician so that everyone could see it and then I popped it seeds and all into my mouth. Carefully I chewed it. I sat there with that cherry pepper exploding in my mouth and scorching my tongue and lips. Tears filled my eyes. I looked at Peggy. Suddenly I forgot the burning pepper and I started to cry because I loved her so much. A moment later I thought of my mother and I was crying for her. At last I cried because my father and I were alone.

"Oh, Paul," said Sally. "That pepper must be terrible."

"It *is* terrible," I said, with a sob.

"I got to hand it to you, Paul," said Joe.

"It's the silliest thing I ever saw," said Peggy. "It really is. The other boys go out for football and basketball. Edmund Hatcher is studying hard to make the honor society. You're the oldest boy in the class, Paul, and all you ever do is eat hot peppers. I don't even know why I watch you. I think I'll tell Miss Riordan on you."

There was no need to tell Miss Riordan. Miss Riordan knew everything about me. I was usually late for school and I did nothing to make up for it when I arrived. I fell so far behind in my work again that I stopped trying to catch up. Miss Riordan sent a note to my father. He tore it up. She sent another note. Finally she made a special visit to the house. I knew when she was coming and so I hid in the cellar.

Miss Riordan spoke to my father without swallowing words. It was a surprising thing to me. After it happened I took a big bold tone with him and trumpeted around for my rights. He listened and watched me with wild eyes and that head cocked like a starved eagle. Suddenly he jumped up and slapped it out of me.

First of all he offered coffee to Miss Riordan. She refused.

"So you came over to tell me the boy's failing?" he said. "You could've saved yourself the trip."

"Paul is always late," said Miss Riordan. "It's only a matter of minutes at times, but it's a poor habit."

"All right. I'll get him out of here earlier."

"And he can't keep his mind on his work. The truth is, he can't seem to get his mind on it in the first place. He was looking out the window so much that I moved him to a desk near the wall."

"And then he looked at the wall."

"Well, yes. Sometimes I have the feeling he's asleep with

his eyes open. These high-school years are important, Mr. Christopher."

"It's one thing at a time with him."

"I don't understand."

"I mean just that. These days it's the harmonica. He sleeps with it under his pillow. Let me tell you exactly. One night I was cleaning the wine barrel in the cellar. The light burned out. I called up for him to bring a bulb. There were no bulbs. I told him to get the one from the bathroom. He brought it down. He was playing the harmonica all the while. The bulb didn't work. Something was wrong in the switch. I sent him up to get a candle. He came down playing the harmonica and holding the candle. I told him to bring the light close to me. I was scraping the inside of the barrel. He was playing and looking the other way. He brought the candle closer. Do you know where he put it? He practically put it in my ear. I hollered and knocked it out of his hand. He ran upstairs. I fell over the barrel and ripped my leg open. I was lying in the dark with my leg bleeding. That ear was like a red-hot bird on my head. It was quiet in the house. And then guess what? I heard him playing the harmonica on the porch. I think it was the same song he was playing before. I tell you the boy's not there!"

"You don't mean that. Isn't it true he works hard? I've heard from one of the girls that he helps a great deal in the house. By the way, Mr. Christopher, I had a feeling there was something on his breath the other morning."

"I let him put whiskey in his coffee when it's cold out. It doesn't hurt him. It warms him up. He never catches cold."

"I wonder."

"You think it'll put a craving in him?"

"I think it makes him light-headed and then drowsy."

"It isn't the whiskey."

"Please don't misunderstand me about Paul. He's a sweet boy and has a very fine mind. All our tests prove it."

"Really?"

"Don't you think so?" she said, sharply. "I try to build his interest by giving him certain responsibilities. I let him collect the test papers and guard the halls during study hours. He helps to stack books in the library and he takes the tickets and watches the door during the noon movie period."

"Very pretty. I'm a watchman because I'm done for. He's just starting out and he's a watchman."

"He does everything but his school work."

"There's no sense in him. It's our fault, too. We were too old when we had him. We lost one son and wanted another."

"Really, Mr. Christopher, I'm shocked to hear you talk like this."

"I'll tell you a secret. He takes after my brother. My brother could talk and make me laugh out loud. And I'm not a laughing man. He could talk and make a woman cry just with his words. The old women in the neighborhood used to come and listen to him so they could cry. I saw it myself. But he couldn't put one foot after another to help himself. Once he bought an old harp. When I told him to look for a job he said he had a job right there learning to play that harp. I sent him back to Italy. He died soon afterward. He didn't belong here or there or anywhere."

"I'm sorry."

"He never even learned to play the harp."

"But each of us belongs somewhere," said Miss Riordan.

"It's words and music with them. They belong to the wind."

"Paul needs understanding."

"That's why he's in school."

"I don't mean that."

"I'll tell you what," said my father. "I'll cut out the whiskey in his coffee and we'll see what happens. How's that?"

"I don't understand you, Mr. Christopher."

"Listen then. Pretty soon he'll be done with schooling and it's a different thing. When I was his age I left my family and my country. I came here and worked in a coal mine. This boy plays the harmonica and forgets where his shoes are. He's beginning to think the harmonica will get him through life. I'm doing what I can for him. He needs food and a place to stay. I'm doing my best. Later he'll need iron in his bones and I've got nothing to do with it."

"But you have everything to do with it. Don't you realize that the death of his mother might have had serious effects on him? No doubt life has been hard for you, Mr. Christopher. Is that a reason to make it hard for your son? It's a good reason to make it as pleasant as possible while you can."

"Talk to me about school and books. Don't talk to me

about life. I've had enough. I don't even know why my heart goes on beating."

"Perhaps it's for your son."

"Will you take a cup of coffee?"

"No, Mr. Christopher, thank you."

"You'll settle for words?"

"You may be right," said Miss Riordan. "There are times when words belong to the wind."

And so she left.

Down in the cellar I made a solemn promise to pay attention and do better in school. Even now it gives me delight when I think of Miss Riordan. Time and again she helped and encouraged me. She spent long hours tutoring me for examinations. True enough that the students mocked her. She was thin as a board and had this habit of looking down sudden and hard at you as though you were a bug. And yet I remember a softer light in those eyes. Now and then I stayed after school to play the harmonica for her while she put papers in order and gathered her books. I was never in any hurry to get home. I would sit at my desk and play song after song for her. No sound could be heard in the building. Sometimes she stopped to look down at me and listen closely. There were precious moments when her eyes would go soft with some remembered love and I played and played with heart pounding inside me as though that love could be saved to light her down dark ways forever.

5

All along I had this feeling our troubles would be over if I managed to graduate from Lincoln High School. I was wrong. A summer of trouble was beginning. My father was right when he said it would be a different thing for me out in the world.

"No one will hold your hand like that teacher," he said. "The harmonica days are over. Now you learn to march."

He heard drumbeats that I never heard.

Right after graduation I went out to look for a job. The newspapers were calling it an interval of economic adjustment and it seemed that during such intervals there was no work to be done. Every morning I shaved and put on a clean shirt and took the bus down to the Public Square. I had high hope even though I spent half of each day filling out long applications to prove I was qualified for nothing. Several employers promised to call and give me a chance when openings occurred. Some were disappointed to hear I had no plans for college. A man called P. P. Peterson studied my application for a while and then called me into his office.

"Let's see now," he said. "Do you want me to tell you how this looks to me? You were probably the oldest boy in your graduating class. You say you were in the lower third of the class and from your grades I'd say you were lucky they didn't divide into tenths. Your last year, however, was very good. Now you don't look strong enough to do any heavy work and at the same time you can't type. I see one of your hobbies is playing the harmonica. Well, Paul, that's something."

"I play well."

"I'm sure you do. At least I hope you do since it's what you do."

He burst into laughter. He brought his left hand down again and again on the huge polished desk. In a moment he regained control of himself. He looked at me as though at an intruder.

"Here's the thing," he said. "I can't pay you for playing the harmonica. Now don't misunderstand me. All this doesn't really matter too much. I wouldn't be afraid to train you up for something. I just don't have a spot for you. But I like your looks and I'd like to give you some advice. Do you mind?"

"I'd appreciate it."

"Never sit down at an interview until you're invited to sit down. Smile once when you introduce yourself. Don't keep smiling and melting away like that in the chair. It looks like you're falling in love with me. Be serious and alert. Pretend there's a bee on the nose of your interviewer. Watch the bee. And now I'd like to wish you good luck. Remember that bee."

It seemed there was a bee in my ear. I heard the same thing everywhere I went. I was getting so discouraged that I started out later in the morning and came home earlier in the afternoon. One morning as I used to do when cutting school I went down in the Terminal Tower to wait for trains. My father had a mysterious first cousin who lived in Vandergrift, Pennsylvania, and so I moved into a crowd of people and looked eager as though expecting him on the next train. There was a deep spreading rumble and then a hot hissing from the level beneath us. The train had arrived. A few minutes later people were climbing the stairs and riding up the escalator. All at once I was caught in the midst of laughter and kissing and tears. I smiled welcome to everyone and most of them smiled and nodded to me. After meeting two more trains I strolled out to sit on a bench in the Public Square. I tossed peanuts to the fat bobbing pigeons. So pleased was I that I bought a cherry pie to please my father. He had developed a taste for sweets since his retirement from work.

Late in the afternoon I went home. An old friend of the family was waiting to see me. His name was Sam Ross. He was sipping wine and puffing a crooked black cigar. He looked me over. He thought it was a wonderful thing that

I graduated from high school. Suddenly he pinched my cheek and slapped me on the knee.

"Look at him," he said. "Look at that brown hair, Carl, and those soft eyes. And that mouth. The picture of his mother, God rest her soul. Isn't it true, Carl?"

"I see the pie and I know it's another wasted day."

"He's found no job yet?" said Sam.

"Ask him," said my father. "He's in front of you."

"Your father never changes," said Sam. "The last time I was here he put the oven higher and higher. 'But what are you cooking?' I said. He was cooking *me,* Paul. He was trying to get rid of me. Why didn't he just tell me to go home?"

"Why do you talk about me?" said my father. "I'm right here."

Sam glanced at him and then turned to study me again. He scratched his chin and puffed that cigar. He thought a while and then offered me a temporary job as an assistant on his watermelon wagon. It sounded very good. All I had to do was sit among the watermelons and pass them out to customers when he brought the horse to a stop in a shady place.

"Why not?" he said. "You'll be earning some money. I'll give you six dollars a day. Wait then. Make it seven. Wait then. I understand you play the harmonica. You can play and let the people know we are there. Make it eight dollars a day."

"Do you call that a job?" said my father. "Do you?"

"What do you call it?" said Sam.

"I call it a waste of time."

"Selling watermelons is a waste of time? I make my living this way. Is eating watermelons a waste of time? How about growing watermelons? Really, Carl, you make no sense."

"It's no job for him!"

"Don't be foolish," said Sam. "The boy is tired from all that studying in school. He should rest his mind a little. Besides, he's earning nothing now. He spends money every day looking for work. It's now he's wasting his time."

"Would you want your own son to work on a watermelon wagon?"

"I don't have a son. I don't even have a daughter."

"I mean if you had a son! What would you do?"

"What would I do?" said Sam. "I'd buy a cannon just to fire a salute. I'd be the happiest man in the world."

"Listen to me. He'll find work if he keeps looking for it. No one who wants work will be without it for long."

"Why don't *you* come out with me?"

"Are you out of your mind?"

"I want company in the day," said Sam. "I'm sick of talking to that horse. Besides, Carl, it will do you good to get out of the house. You live in the past here. You look back and back and you don't even see what's in front of you."

"I see what's in front of me. That's why I look back. Now leave me alone."

"In the end we're all left alone. Either to live or die. As for Paul, he can look for another job while he's with me.

He can go whenever he pleases. Meanwhile he'll be earning eight dollars a day. He can help you with the bills here."

"I get my pension and the social security. It's more than enough. The house is paid for. I don't need help from anyone."

"I wish you would come out with me," said Sam. "I'll give you nine dollars a day. Paul plays the harmonica, it's true, but you talk nonsense that's better than music. By the way, how is Nina?"

"They leave when the ship is sinking."

"And you want them to sink," said Sam.

"You've got an answer for everything. Who sent for you?"

"Do you want me to talk here or look out the windows? And why don't you wash the windows? And look at the plaster falling."

"Put your own house in order!"

"I pay a woman to put it in order. And I pay a terrible price."

They argued for another hour. In the end Sam had his way by insisting it would be a most practical thing for me to take the job and earn some money until I found work more suitable to my education and natural powers. Meanwhile I could rest my mind a little.

So it was that three days later I went out with Sam Ross for the first time. He had his wagon loaded at the wholesale fruit exchange on Woodland Avenue and then he came to pick me up on the South Side. We traveled around the city.

I played the harmonica and Sam called out that watermelons were for sale.

"Eat and drink and wash your face!" he said.

Children came running and laughing. Their mothers followed them. Everyone was delighted to see us and it seemed a wonderfully perfect way to make a living. All that day we were out in the fresh air and sunlight. Round us was the sweetness of watermelon like cut grass. Deep in the gold of afternoon we sold out and I lay back in the wagon to watch the sky and listen to the quickening clip-clop of the horse Tina.

"She knows when she's going home," said Sam.

He was urging her on and laughing at her. He had a golden front tooth. Laughing now, his brown eyes were lost in a web of wrinkles and his mouth curved toward ears aslant as though in sudden glee. That flashing tooth of gold seemed to tell while keeping the rare secret of laughter. It was good to be with Sam on that watermelon wagon.

The job, however, troubled everyone in Lincoln Court. At first the neighbors gaped at me in utter bewilderment. I didn't understand and so I gaped back at them. Meanwhile my father was muttering and scratching his head. Nina scolded me on the telephone. Peggy Haley thought it was the worst thing that happened since the war. She came over to tell me about it.

"You should be ashamed of yourself," she said.

"What for?"

"I think it's awful," she said. "Selling watermelons!"

"Awful? What's so awful about it? What is this? Do you know what you're talking about?"

"Yes. Everyone is saying the same thing."

"Really? At the same time? Well, I'll tell you what. I'll make a song out of it and then everyone can sing together. What's awful about selling watermelons? People sell all kinds of things. Tell me one thing better than watermelons."

"Anything. Anything is better than going through the streets like that in a wagon. And with a horse. Everybody sees you there."

"And we see everybody."

"Listen a minute, Paul. Think of the other boys we went to school with. Some of those boys are getting ready to go to college. Look at Edmund Hatcher."

"Is his nose bleeding again? Does it still bleed when he gets excited? Does he still carry two handkerchiefs everywhere?"

"For your information, Edmund works for the Midwestern National Bank. They're training him. They're training him for an important position in the credit department. And he goes to business school at night. He's ambitious."

"So am I."

"Are you?"

"Of course I am. I'd like to kiss your lower lip. On both sides of that line. It looks like it was kissed up into two ripe little portions. And both delicious. It's a beautiful mouth, Peggy. Now about this job. I think it's a good job for the summer."

"And what will you do this winter?"

"Save my strength for next summer. The melons might be heavier."

"You just don't understand. You're getting off on the wrong foot. You'll never live this down, Paul. Everyone is laughing at you."

"Is that true?"

"Every word of it. Believe me."

"Don't you know Sam Ross has been doing this for years and years? He makes so much money in the summer he doesn't lift a finger all winter. He's got this big open fireplace at home. He burns these logs and warms his feet and looks for faces in that fire. While the wind blows and the snow piles up."

"Is that all he does?"

"Now he's got something else to do. He can laugh. He can laugh at all the people who laugh at him in the summer. I'm going to tell him to look for their faces in the fire. You'll be on the list."

"It's a job for little boys and old men! You're just starting out in life. What'll happen when you go looking for a job and tell them you've been selling watermelons? From a wagon in the street? Well? What's your ambition in life?"

"I want a wagon of my own."

"Stop it, Paul."

"And a white horse. With plumes as black as your hair."

"I don't even know why I'm talking to you."

"I know why. You came to hear the secret."

"Secret?" she said, alerted. "What secret?"

"Come closer. I'll whisper it. Look at this. Do you know

your ear is like a little hidden wing? So pretty and still with your hair waving and curving around it. Now there's another secret. Do you know what the first one is? I'd like to whisper secrets in your ear."

"And the second one?"

"I love you."

"Oh, Paul," she said, blushing.

"I wish I had a plum."

"A plum?"

"I'm teasing. Really, Peggy, I love you with all my heart. I used to spend whole days in school watching your hair. And your ear. And the curve of your neck. It was enough for me. Why, I thought there was nothing more in the world. And then guess what? Remember that day a long time ago when I fell out of my desk and cut my head? Miss Goldberg thought I fainted."

"I think I remember. Yes, Paul, I do remember."

"I was watching you that day. I guess your leg was itching. You reached down to scratch it and your dress came up. I saw your leg above the knee. It was so soft and white and beautiful that tears came in my eyes. What more could I ask? I was just getting over it and you started scratching again. You were squirming and scratching and your dress was coming up higher and higher and I was leaning forward there and my heart popped in my mouth! All at once I saw the curve of your bottom! I couldn't catch my breath! It looked like a honeydew melon at first! And then the breast of a swan! And then like a big pearl! And I could only see the beginning of it! And it looked like there was no end to it! I was leaning and leaning and I fell forward on my head!"

"Paul!" she was saying, blushing hotly. "Paul!"

"What a reward for all my watching! I spent the rest of the year in that ancient history class waiting for you to scratch your leg again. I mean it. I missed two thousand years of history. And I'm still waiting. Do it before you go home."

"You must be crazy, Paul. I never heard such things."

"I want to marry you as soon as possible. I can't stand it much longer. And then I'll be in a position to scratch your leg. Really, Peggy, I love everything about you. I always did. I always will."

"You shouldn't be saying these things. You really shouldn't."

"Why shouldn't I? It's how I feel about you. Don't you hear me playing the harmonica at night? Sometimes I'm playing it just for you. And I make up songs for you, too. It's the truth. How about it if I come over and sit on your porch later? We'll make some plans. I'll bring a surprise for you."

"A surprise? What is it?"

"A watermelon."

"A watermelon?"

"As red as your lips. And maybe as sweet. I doubt it. But I'll find out later."

"Keep your old watermelon!"

"Don't you like watermelon?"

"You're hopeless, Paul. You really and truly are."

She left me there on the porch.

In the following days I found out that she was right about the neighbors. They whispered and laughed at me when I walked through the alley. I used to whistle or play the harmonica and everyone would wave and say hello. Now it was different.

"It's the watermelon boy," one would say.

"Say, Paul, does that horse eat watermelon?"

"Do you ever look that horse in the eye, Paul?"

"Tell me something," said the barber Regas. "Just one thing. How can I tell if a melon is sweet?"

"Tap it," I said. "Tap it on the left side."

"The left side? Which is the left side?"

"It's the side in your left hand. Tap it and listen close."

"And then?"

"Cut it open and taste it."

Regas laughed and laughed. Along with everyone he was laughing when that joke was forgotten. I started to slip out of the house like a thief and walk over to Scranton Avenue to meet Sam Ross. Laughter in the alley went a little hard with mockery and seemed to follow me everywhere. It followed my father closer. He was brooding until he turned completely against that job. Just about then I surprised him by going downtown to pay the semi-annual tax on the house. It came to ninety dollars. He thought it over and held it against me as though I had moved to undermine his remaining power and authority. He sat on the porch and blew up a cloud of pipe smoke when he saw me coming from work with a watermelon lifted like a prize in the palm of my hand.

Day after day I brought watermelon home. I brought quarters and halves and then for Sunday I brought a whole one. The refrigerator was loaded. I tried to eat as much as I was bringing. I would have a big smiling cut of it for supper. After cleaning the kitchen I played the harmonica. Music gave me a taste for more melon. I ate another piece and it washed me so fresh and clean inside that I played the harmonica again. Before going to bed I ate another piece of melon. Around three in the morning I woke to eat again. It was like a spell on me. My shirts and trousers and underclothes were stained with juice. I found seeds in my pockets and shoes. It seemed that whenever I turned around my father was watching me spit seeds idly into the garbage pail in front of my chair. There were times in the evening when the only sound was the tick of seeds against the sides of that metal pail. Toward the end I think my father was coming awake at three in the morning to stare in the dark and listen to the dry tick of seeds.

My talk failed to help the situation.

"This piece isn't bad," I would say. "It's better than the one I had yesterday. Still, the one I had Monday was best of all. I wish I could find another melon like that. I was eating and wondering what was missing. I was eating and wondering and eating and wondering. And then it was gone and I knew what was missing. The piece was perfect and it was the rest of the melon that was missing. . . . Have we got time for some music before supper? It'll do you good."

My father turned sullen. He didn't talk much and to spite me he wouldn't eat any watermelon. He would open the refrigerator and stand there with eyes blazing and that pipe aiming straight from his mouth. One afternoon I came into the yard with half a melon held high in my hand. He was sitting in the rocker on the porch. He was holding the sides of that chair as though to keep it from falling apart. His knuckles bulged into white marbles.

"What's that?" he said, though he could see it plain.

"Half a melon. It's a beauty, Pa."

"We don't have enough yet?"

The next afternoon I came home with another half. He was waiting for me in the kitchen. I started talking to cheer him after his lonely day. I wanted to tease him just to hear his quick sour laughter.

"Sam says I'm doing fine," I said. "He may raise my salary. One thing sure, he'll be giving me a whole watermelon every night. He says he'll stay ahead of us if it's the last thing he ever does. Not a half or a quarter, Pa. It'll be a whole one every day. But I don't want you to worry. I've got it all figured out. I'll take a day off work every week to eat and catch up with him."

I opened the refrigerator. Watermelon bulged from every shelf.

"We should buy another refrigerator," I said. "Now let's eat a piece of melon before putting this piece in. I'll take a half out to make room for this half. But I see you didn't eat any today. What a naughty boy you are. Do you know a strange thing is happening to me? It seems like all I think about is watermelon."

"And it's all I think about," he said, softly.

"Do you know what happened about three this morning?"

"And it's all I think about," he was saying, even more softly.

"I was eating this piece of melon and when I finished it the bottom of the pail was black with seeds. Now listen to this. A watermelon grows from one seed. Isn't that right? But there'll be a hundred seeds in the watermelon that grew from one seed. This means each watermelon has enough seeds to give a hundred watermelons. And these watermelons have enough seeds for thousands and thousands. And then millions and millions. What does this mean? I was thinking about it. I was thinking maybe God wanted to make sure there'd be enough watermelons so that everyone everywhere would have them until the end of the world. Plant all those wasted seeds and in a few years we'd have watermelons piled up into whole ranges of mountains. Why, it's just like God was planning a big feast where everyone sits and eats watermelon. Sam says there's no end to it."

"Sam is wrong!" cried my father. "Sam is wrong! There'll be an end to it! I'm making an end right now!"

He tore open the refrigerator. He pounced on those melons and started throwing them out the window and door. Melons went flying through the air to split open on the porch and in the yard. Neighbors gathered. Peggy was there. My father threw out every piece but the one on the table. I picked it up. I was so excited that I threw it out the window to join him in the uproar.

"So much for Sam!" he cried. "And so much for God's

plans again! It's the end of the watermelons! Do you understand? And I'm sick of this job! Everyone's laughing at you! You're making a jackass out of yourself! And me, too!"

"Maybe we should talk this over."

"Why did I work all these years? So you could sell watermelons from a wagon? Is that it? Wake up! You live in a country where you can be anything you want and look what the hell you're doing! You're going backward full speed! The next thing I know you'll be sailing back to the old country to herd sheep! Get out! And clean up that mess out there!"

I swept up those broken melons and threw several pails of water to keep flies away. Afterward I sat on the porch step. My father stormed around the house until dark and then he came out to rock his fury away in the chair at the other end of the porch. There was the red glow of steel mill fire in the sky. Smokestacks seemed to be bobbing like black masts out of a midnight harbor. Sudden white smoke billowed from a distant stack and for an instant froze in a kind of fairyland tower in the dark. Now I heard the rhythmic creak of the rocking chair. I played the harmonica with it. My father rocked a little faster to free the creak of the chair from my song. I played faster. Suddenly he was rocking so fast that I stopped playing. I burst into laughter. His hair was white as the smoke and he was bowing and rearing in that chair as though astride some runaway horse in the night.

Time and again my father warned me that men lost power when they talked too much. I told him he was losing power in telling me about it and he said he started to lose power the day I spoke my first word.

"It's in the family," I said. "You must be losing it to me."

"And you lose it to everyone," he said.

He was right. I told everyone in Lincoln Court about my next job even before I started to work. I had this interview with the personnel director of the Big Deal grocery store chain. His name was John Whipple and he offered to put me on a training course that would qualify me in four weeks to work as an assistant butcher in any Big Deal store in the country. He took such a fancy to me that he spent an hour telling me the story of his rise to success. He traced that success to perseverance and loyalty.

"An ounce of loyalty is worth a pound of cleverness," he said.

"Yes, sir."

"Now I see you've been selling watermelons."

"It was a sort of a temporary job."

"It means you've been dealing with the public. It's the hardest thing in the world. What do you make of the American people?"

"Well, they like watermelon."

"I like you, Paul," he said. "You've been watching me like a hawk. You're alert and you've had experience that might be helpful. We want young men like you. We want men with potential for growth. We want you to grow with the company. We're building new stores all the time. All over the world. And it isn't just to sell food for a profit. That's the obvious reason. Our president, G. W. Whitcomb, sees it in another light. Mr. Whitcomb says the American people may not be thinking straight or even thinking at all. But they have energy and they need food. We'll be everywhere to supply good clean food to keep this energy at a high level. Until the wonderful things happen."

"The wonderful things?"

"The wonderful things this energy will create."

"When do I start work, Mr. Whipple?"

"Good boy. Then you want to be part of this?"

"Yes, sir."

"I know I can count on you. I knew it the minute I saw you. Now don't let me down. We're on the wing here. Learn how to fly."

"I'll learn, sir."

"Think you'll be happy in this organization?"

"I know I will."

"You're hired, Paul Christopher."

I would train for one month in the main cooler and then work as an assistant butcher in the Big Deal store on the South Side. Promotions would follow fast. I thanked John Whipple and left him. I hurried over to that store on the South Side and told the manager Horace P. Willis that I would soon be working in his meat department.

"Welcome aboard," he said, smiling.

Horace took me on a tour of that supermarket. It was almost as large as Lincoln Park. Above there was light enough to turn midnight into noon. Nothing was hidden. Rows and rows of stainless-steel shelves were loaded with fruit and vegetables and canned goods. It was a feast of color. All the employees wore white uniforms and white hats. They were smiling and smiling until it seemed there would be a sudden tremendous wave of laughter sweeping through that store. I talked for a while with the chief butcher Herman Bauer. He kept squeezing my hand like a sponge. He was eager to have me with him. I was so delighted that I went out and told everyone in the alley about the new job.

It was too soon to start work the very next day. I had put it off until the following week just to enjoy thinking and talking about it. Sam Ross wished me luck and reminded me that I could go out with him whenever I wanted. My father seemed pleased by the news.

"I'll learn how to cut meat in one month," I told him. "But it's only the first step on the ladder."

"Look out the first step isn't loose."

"I'll be an assistant butcher for a while and then pretty soon I'll be in charge of that meat department."

"Pretty soon? It's in the same sentence."

"I'll be waiting for you, Pa. Come and find me. I'll be wearing a white uniform and a white hat like a big marsh-mallow. And I'll have a badge with my picture and name on it. Guess what?"

"There's more? Besides the badge?"

"I was talking to the butcher Herman Bauer. He told me to smile when they take my picture for that badge. Everybody remembers a smiling face. And he told me to be polite to customers. Sometimes a customer praises you to the manager. When it happens the manager puts a gold star by your name. And when you get a lot of stars he calls you in."

"What happens?"

"What happens? He showers you with stars and gives you a kiss. What do you think happens? He promotes you. Why, I'll smile myself into a store of my own in no time. And then I can laugh a little. Come and find me, Pa. I'll be the one counting stars. Now there's something else. This Herman Bauer must be well over sixty years old. You'd think he was a wreck."

"You mean I'd know it."

"I wish you'd go over and see him. What a picture of health. He put his hand on me like a clamp. What strength.

And why not? He eats the best of everything. Every night he takes home a pound of the choice cuts of meat. It's not allowed but everybody looks the other way."

"Everybody steals and so nobody's a thief."

"Herman told me he planned to work until he was eighty years old and then he'll play for twenty years."

"At what? Living?"

"I was looking at the picture on his badge. I couldn't believe it was the same man. I looked at Herman and at the picture and at Herman. What a change since he started work in that store. From a lamb to a lion. I couldn't believe it was the same man."

"Well?"

"It wasn't the same man, Pa. The picture on the badge was a picture of his brother who died two years ago. They worked together. Herman lost his own badge and he's wearing his brother's until he gets a new one. Guess what? I told him to smile when they take his picture."

"I think I've had enough of you for a while."

"Mr. Whipple was right. I've been on the wing since I left him. I think I'll fly over and tell Peggy the good news."

Peggy was waiting for me on the porch step. She smiled and the light in her eyes whispered an invitation to be sweet and then cruel and then sweeter still in the night. An excitement gripped me as though I heard the sudden pounding music of a parade. I started to talk about the silver of moon and stars beyond the smoke. She interrupted to talk about my new job.

"I heard about it," she said. "It sounds very nice."

"Doesn't it? He's putting me under this course of training. It won't be long now. He says he'll have me off the streets in no time."

"It's a job with a future."

"I'll end up as the manager of one of those Big Deal stores."

"I don't see why not."

"Neither do I. I really don't. They may even send me to open a store in Mexico or South America. Come with me, Peggy. I'll be wearing a white uniform and a white hat like a chef. I'll tell everybody I'm going somewhere to cook for a king."

"You'll look cute, Paul."

"Say my name again, Peggy."

"Don't you hear it enough?"

"Not like that. And I never even hear it at home. I wonder if my father forgot it. I'll remind him."

"Paul then. Paul, Paul."

For a long moment we were watching each other in the night. A light went on behind us in the kitchen. I touched her hand and we stood up. We strolled out of the alley and around the corner to Lincoln Park. It was deserted. Wind was stealing softly through the leaves of maple and sycamore. Holding my breath, I leaned over to kiss her hand. She turned to me and we kissed under the trees. Her clinging lips were moist on mine. Her body was ripe and sweet and willing. Her breasts were pressing all round my heart. I kissed her lips again and again. Suddenly they opened for me and that hot sweet rush of breath took my own away. I was melting inside with love and longing for her. In the same moment it flashed through my mind that this was a much better thing than playing the harmonica.

We sat on a park bench near the playground and swimming pool. We looked around as though waiting to be introduced to each other. Foolishly, I started to talk again.

"When I start work in that store, Peggy, I'll bring a surprise for you every day. Do you know they have lobster from South Africa?"

"It sounds dreamy."

"And peas and potatoes from Belgium. Those potatoes are like little white marbles."

We strolled back and sat on her porch. All was dark and quiet in the house. We twined our fingers and kissed again and again. I kissed her pale eyes and dark fragrant hair. Soon I was exploring the milky pulsing warmth of her throat. No longer could I keep my hands away from the curving places of her body.

"You shouldn't," she whispered. "Please, Paul."

"But I should. You mean I mustn't."

"Well then, you mustn't."

"My darling Peggy. But why don't we do it?"

"You don't mean it."

"I do mean it. I love you and I want to marry you."

"Is that what you mean?"

"I mean everything. I mean business. Let's get married on the day after I get my first pay."

"Why do you get so serious? How can you say such a thing?"

"I say what I feel. What do you want me to say?"

"You don't have any plans or anything. It's just words."

"Plans for what?"

"For what? For everything. Where would we live?"

"Where would we live? We'd live in my house."

"Are you serious, Paul?"

"Of course I'm serious. Why do you keep saying that? It's like you're asking if I'm in my right mind."

"Well, are you? Do you expect me to live in Lincoln Court?"

"Of course. What's wrong with Lincoln Court? It's where you do live. What's the matter with you?"

"Is this a place for children to grow up in?"

"I don't understand. It's the place if it's where they are."

"I see."

"What is this, Peggy? Children grow up wherever they are. Children are like flowers."

"Then you don't see anything wrong in having your children here? And living the rest of your life here?"

"What's wrong with it?"

"What's right with it?"

"Your mother and father are here. You were born here. And it's a good thing they didn't feel like you do. Where would you be?"

"I'm not going to die here, Paul."

"You mean you're looking for a better place to die? I

don't understand this. What difference does it make where we live?"

"All right then. What would we live on?"

"But I've got this wonderful job."

"You didn't even start yet. Is this what you offer a girl?"

"What is all this? I love you. I'll take care of you always. I can do a lot of things. I can cook and wash clothes and clean house. I know how to shop for food. I'm good-natured and I make up songs. Ask anyone about Paul Christopher."

"You don't understand how things are with me. Do you really expect me to spend the rest of my life in this smoke and dirt? I watched my mother get old and gray in this alley. I won't let it happen to me."

"But where is this other place you're talking about? This place where the children are supposed to be and nobody gets gray? Is it in the city limits? It must be one of those new suburbs. Is it Parma Heights? I heard taxes were high there."

"I don't want to discuss it with you."

"Let me tell you a story. They say my uncle used to tell it. Once upon a time there was an old man. He was sitting in a chair and all he had left in the world was a pile of old strings and some pieces of wood. Now his chair was uncomfortable and he complained about it. And then he complained about the room the chair was in and then the house the room was in. And then he complained about the street where the house was and then the city and then the world. Do you know what they did? They put a cushion on his chair. And then he didn't know what to say and so he took the old strings and those pieces of wood and he made himself a harp. And then he began to make music for everyone who came to the house. And then he made music for the city and the world. Do you know what I think? I'll have to find a cushion for the chair of my darling Peggy."

"There's just no use talking to you. Good night."

"Wait then. How about another kiss?"

"No."

"Wait then. At least scratch your leg before you go. Think of it. Two thousand years of history lost."

"You're impossible, Paul. Now I'm sure of it."

She went in and closed the door.

I walked home. My father was sitting in the rocker on the porch. He was smoking his pipe. For a moment it troubled me to see him sitting alone in the night. Suddenly I felt sure he had been waiting for me to come home and talk and tease him a little. I wanted to give him the delight that Peggy had given me.

"Well, sir, we meet again," I said. "I'd like to remind you that my name is Paul. I stopped by to let you know it won't be long now."

"For what?"

"Three more days and I start work on that new job."

"That's why I'm up. I was waiting to hear more about it."

"This will be a wonderful year. First I'll get married. And then I'll paint the house. I'll borrow that aluminum ladder from Theodore Ampazis. He says I can lift it with one finger. I'll paint the house white and then I'll start on the inside. I'll plaster the cracks in the walls and paint every room. And then I'll buy a car and we'll take long rides down along the lake in the evening. Do you know what? I've been thinking about your cousin in Vandergrift, Pennsylvania. In fact, I was waiting for him the other day. What's his name?"

"Michael. Michael Christopher."

"We should take a trip this summer and surprise Michael."

"Are you losing your mind? I never saw the man. I don't know anything about him. What the hell do I want to see him for?"

"Just for those reasons. Don't you wonder about him? Don't you ever think about his life? Is he married? Has he got any children? How does he earn his living? Does he like music? Does he walk in the woods at night and listen for the song of the nightingale? Are there any nightingales in Vandergrift? Listen, Pa, listen."

"There's no choice for me."

"It's Michael Christopher! He's calling in the night. Hello, Michael, hello! Speak, Michael, speak! Tell us what you want us to do. Your cousin is waiting, Michael. Not your third cousin. Not your second cousin. It's your first cousin and you can tell him everything. . . . Do you know what, Pa? I'm going to make a song for Michael Christopher and his family. Would you like to hear it?"

"Play if you want to play. It's either talk or music with you."

"Isn't it strange? I can't stop thinking about Michael.

What do you think he's doing right this minute? Is he waiting for the song?"

"I'll tell you what he's doing. He's sitting there scratching his head. He's wondering where it all started and where it will end. And he's wondering what the hell it all means."

7

By the time I started work on that new job I had promised to bring special chops and roasts and sausages to most of the neighbors. They invited me to join them for supper on those occasions. I told Theodore Ampazis that I would bring him a leg of lamb every Saturday.

"We'll eat it on Sunday," he said. "I'll roast it for you with garlic and parsley and origan. And bay leaf and dill. Then I'll make some rice for you in the juice. And it won't be like smashed potatoes. You'll be able to count this rice. And then maybe you'll play the harmonica for me."

"It sounds good," I said. "I'll be eating like a king around here. I'm supposed to bring Florio some round steak sliced very thin. He'll put special things in it and then roll it up and tie it with a string. He'll cook it for three hours in tomato sauce. After that I'll have supper with Sophie Nowak. She'll make a pork roast or sausage with sauerkraut."

"Is your father satisfied with this job?" said Theodore.

"He says the first step on the ladder is loose."

It turned out that my father was right. I was thinking and talking so much about the job that I was bound to be disappointed. Truth be told I was more disappointing than disappointed.

Early Monday morning the man in charge of trainees at the main cooler made a speech to six of us about the door of opportunity. His name was Martin and he moved around us as though his shoes were hot. He kept talking about the door of opportunity while we washed our hands with a strong pine soap and put on white aprons and white hats.

"The door of opportunity is locked," said Martin. "The lock on that door is a combination lock. The combination to that lock is hard work, loyalty, honesty, and hard work. Nothing else will spring the lock on that door."

He opened a high, wide, heavy door. It led into the cooler. He stationed two of us at each of three wooden chopping blocks and showed us an assortment of shining knives. He explained that we were to get the feel of butchering by trimming meat off beef bones. The meat would be ground into hamburger or chopped into stew. It would be delivered that very day to Big Deal stores throughout the city and then sold the next day in weighed and priced packages.

"Now pay attention," said Martin. "These bones must be clean as a hound's tooth. I mean when they leave your hands. They should look like the lions finished up on them. Trim off every bit of meat and fat and then drop the bones in these barrels. There's a barrel for each one of you. Try to fill your barrel with white bones. You'll see rib bones and neck bones. Chine bones and knuckle bones. White bones, white bones. Do you understand?"

"Yes, sir," I said.

Everyone glanced at me.

"But I want you to be careful," said Martin. "Take your time. Don't cut yourself. Find the best way to get at the meat. Sometimes you'll come in at the top and cut down. Sometimes you'll get in from underneath or slice away at the sides. Get the feel of working with these knives. Try them all. You'll do it wrong for a while. I'll be back as soon as I can to show you how it should be done. One thing more. You'll come out of the cooler every hour or so for a five-minute relief. Now let's get with it."

Martin went out. The tremendous door closed. It closed on a precise delicate click that seemed to send shivers through the walls to be sure we were sealed perfectly in that iron room. I felt sealed. I put the feeling out of my mind and turned to the work. I lifted a big bone to my chopping block and started to trim the red meat away. It took me an hour to strip that cold heavy bone. I kept turning it around and finding more meat. At last I dropped it into the barrel. I saw strands of meat on it and took it out of the barrel. I went over and over it. Martin failed to mention that the meat belongs on the bone.

I was taking that same bone out of the barrel for the third time when Martin came through the door. He moved around and watched for a while and then he told us to stop and watch him.

"Come closer," he said.

He picked up a bone from the center block and swung it over to my chopping block. His control of it was perfect. He set it down without a sound. He rubbed his hands together as for a feast and then he started to sharpen knives one on the other. His hands flew like birds and the clean thin whistling of blade on blade was all round us in the cold air. He put one knife aside and studied the flashing blade of the other. Now he was going into a kind of secret menacing dance like a swordsman. He moved in to make a series of quick deep overhand cuts down along that bone. It was impossible to follow his knife. It was everywhere at once. Meat was falling and falling. In no time at all he stripped that bone so white it might have dried in the sun. It was a remarkable thing. I had an urge to pounce on that bone and hide it in my barrel.

"Get the idea?" he said. "Attack, attack."

"Wonderful," I said.

Everyone glanced at me.

"And now it's your turn," said Martin, dropping the bone in my barrel. "Dig in there. Cut deep. Strip it away. Lions, lions."

He went out.

I took another bone and started to cut the meat away. I stopped to sharpen my knives. I was sharpening those knives and listening to the whistling round my head like a flight of silver arrows. I studied the blade and then danced in to cut the meat. After a while I wanted to hear that whistling again and so I stopped to sharpen the knives. My hands and arms were beginning to ache a little.

I dropped the bone into my barrel and lifted another to the block. I was sharpening knives when the cooler door opened. Martin came in to inspect the bones in each barrel. He took the three bones out of mine.

"This one's all right," he said.

"I think it's very good," I said.

"Do you?"

"It's the one you did."

"Then you know what I want. Take charge of these bones. Scrape them clean. You'll have to do better than this."

At noon a distant siren called us to lunch. We marched out of the cooler. I ate a salami sandwich and a cherry pepper. Afterward I went outside to sit on the front step. A soft breeze was stirring the leaves of the willow tree on the lawn. White clouds drifted on the blue sky. The sleepy warmth of noon was stealing through me. Suddenly the raw ugly blast of the siren ripped into the air right above my head.

I went back to my block in the cooler. I looked around while sharpening my knives. The men seemed to be working faster. They were trying to fill their barrels with bones before the day ended. It was good to watch them work. The man across from me would lift a bone to his block and slap the bulge of meat with his hand in a reckless way. Sometimes he slapped it twice to show his contempt. The man beside him was an artist. He moved as though on tiptoe and then lunged to risk everything on a single daring cut. Sudden white bone thrilled him. He had reached through to the hidden beauty. The man at my block would cut and slash until it seemed he would throw the knife aside and tear the meat off with his hands. Once I heard him growling.

More and more often Martin came in to take bones out of barrels and inspect them. He kept finding scraps of meat.

"Look here," he said. "Look at this. Here's a bone with two or three ounces of meat on it. Maybe more. What if you do twenty bones a day like this? You'll be wasting over three pounds of meat. Every day. Do you know what that amounts to in a month? In a year? I'll bet it runs to a ton of waste. Get with it."

I asked him for another demonstration. He gave me a hard stabbing look while he sharpened the knives. He was studying the edge of one of those blades and then a moment later he was looking past it into my eyes. Suddenly his chin came down on his chest and he was dancing again as he moved in to cut quick and deep into that meat. His knife was flashing everywhere like a silver fire. Meat was falling away and hitting the block. All at once the bone was alone. Martin lifted it and turned it so we could study it. He presented it to me.

"Attack," he said. "Nothing to it."

I was watching him in amazement. Not a drop of blood was on his apron. His hands were opening and closing.

"Now it's your turn," he said.

He was looking at me.

From then on he concentrated on me. He came through

that door and over to my block as though I had sent for him.

"You handle that knife like a girl," he said. "And you touch the meat like it's hot. Take hold."

Once I put the knife down when I went over to get a bone. I swung the bone to the block and then reached for the knife. It was gone. I looked on the block and on the floor. I was looking and looking until Martin came over and lifted the bone. The knife was there. I giggled in a foolish way. Martin didn't smile.

"You work pretty slow," he said.

"I'll do better."

"Four bones in five hours. Some of these boys did more than ten. And not one of yours was really right the first time."

"I'll get this one right."

"You can't talk the meat off the bone."

"No, sir."

"Show me what you can do."

I was sharpening the knives as he went through the door. He heard the whistling of those blades and he glanced over his shoulder. We were watching each other as the door closed.

The air seemed to be turning colder. Everyone was digging and slashing away. Aprons had gone dark with blood. Bones thumped into the barrels. I was thinking about the watermelon wagon and the old brown horse Tina. I remembered my first long look at Tina. Her great body sagged as though with the pity flooding my heart and then her body swelled as though with the big yell of laughter inside me. Thinking of her put an ache in my heart.

Martin came in again. Ruthlessly he plunged into my barrel. He counted the same four bones. He looked bewildered.

"You still on the same bone?" he said.

"I guess so."

"What's the matter with you?"

"I've just about got this one."

"Step it up, boy, step it up. You'll have to do better than this. Cut loose now."

"Yes, sir."

My right hand had gone numb. I switched the knife to my left hand. Now it was very hard to cut that meat. A kind of panic was growing in me. I was watching and waiting for Martin. Right about then I felt sure that one clean bone would save the day for me. I decided to steal a bone from the barrel of my neighbor. I would wait until he went over to the center block.

The cooler door was opening.

So frightening was it that I made a quick stab at my bone. I missed it. I cut myself down at the base of my right thumb. I dropped the bone into the barrel and closed my hand while it filled with blood. I put the hand inside my apron.

Martin came right over and lifted the bone out of the barrel. He took the other knife. His chin dropped on his chest and his eyes went narrow as he started to slash away at that bone. All at once there was about a pound of meat on the block. Martin turned to me. His dark eyes were snapping.

"Let's see your hand," he said.

I showed him my hand.

"Put that knife down," he said. "Before you kill yourself. Or get this boy beside you."

I put the knife down.

"Come with me," he said

I felt sick. I followed him through the door. I was looking at my thumb and when he stopped outside I bumped into him. I stained his apron with blood.

"What the hell's wrong with you?" he said.

"I'm very sorry."

He took me into his office where I washed my hand. He put iodine on the cut and bandaged it for me.

"If you cut beef as deep as that you'd be all right," he said.

"I guess so."

"Take the apron off."

I slipped out of the apron and started to fold it neatly. He took it away from me and then he swept off my white hat.

"Your apron is cleaner than your bones," he said. "You're afraid to get some blood on you."

"I'm trying my best."

"Are you?"

"I really am."

"So much the worse," he said. "I don't think you'll work

out on this job. I'm letting you go. I'll mail you a check for the day."

"I'm sorry I couldn't do better."

"Well, it's all right," he said, gently. "Don't feel too bad about it. This work doesn't suit you. I can tell. You should be doing something else. What were you doing before this?"

"I was selling watermelons on a wagon."

"Horse and wagon?"

"Yes, sir."

"Don't see many of them these days. That's a good job for you."

"I'd like to tell you something."

"Go ahead, boy. Have your say. Get it off your chest while you're here. You think I've been dogging you?"

"It isn't that."

"What is it then?"

"Well, never mind."

"Speak up. You'll be sorry you didn't."

"Well, I don't know. It's just that I enjoyed watching you cut that meat. It was really something to see."

"Is that so?" he said, studying me.

"I wish I had enough nerve to ask you to do it again before I go. I'd like to see it once more. I really would."

"You kidding me in some way?"

"Why should I do that?"

"I don't know," he said. "I don't know."

He gave me a long look. He scratched his chin and then he took me back inside the cooler. He swung a big bone to my chopping block. He was watching me as he picked up two knives and started to sharpen them. He put one knife aside. Now he was moving around as though to find sure footing. During that moment he was watching me so close that he danced around to the side of the block. Suddenly he moved in to cut the meat. His knife was flashing here and there and everywhere. Meat was falling away. It seemed he never touched the bone at all.

I held the door open for him and followed him out.

"Are you satisfied?" he said.

"Yes, sir. Thank you very much."

He studied me.

"Wait a minute," he said.

He went back into the cooler. He came out with a white package.

"Here's some stew meat for you," he said.

I thanked him and we shook cold hands.

8

I stopped at the coffee house to tell Theodore about the job. He leaned on the cracked marble counter and listened to me. Brown strands of hair went all astray on his swollen egg of a head. Smoky brown eyes were buried behind the bloom of nose. His sunken cheeks were pitted like peach stones.

The card players kept calling to him.

"A cup of coffee, Theodore," said Regas. "One more thing. Take off your mask when you bring it."

"They say Socrates was an ugly man, too," said Poulos.

"Socrates is dead," said Regas. "We listen to him but we don't have to sit and look at him. Theodore is a slap in the face to every living Greek. A man could look and look at that face. He could think for a thousand years and never guess that a Greek ever had a dream about a beautiful thing."

Theodore was waiting for me to continue my story. I finished it and showed him the package of stew meat and the bandage around my thumb. He started to laugh. He cupped his hand over his mouth to hide the gap of two missing front teeth. He laughed tears into his eyes. He told the gamblers about my experience in the cooler. They filled the coffee house with bursts of laughter. It sounded like a triumph for me. Some of those Greeks nodded and waved welcome to me. They took delight in things going wrong.

After a moment of silence we heard the bubbling laughter of Marko who sat alone in the corner. It seemed the news had just reached him. His hands were on his knees and he leaned forward to laugh and laugh.

"Was it that funny?" I said. "Maybe he should go over and tell my father about it. I wish he would, Theodore."

"He's not laughing at you. Marko's a little loose."

"Loose?"

"Someone said he's got the limit. He fell off a bridge while he was painting. He broke almost every bone in his body. They say he remembers falling all the way. And now he laughs and laughs."

"But why?"

"Who knows? I asked him once and he laughed harder. Listen, Paul, don't worry about that job. Go back on the wagon till you find something you like to do. And take your father a *baclava*. Sweeten him up before you tell him what happened."

My father was sitting in the kitchen. To alert him I put the package of stew on the table and kept my hand on it a moment so that he would get a good look at the bandage. He was looking at that bandage as though at a little crushed white bird in my hand. I found myself turning my hand so that he could see it from all sides.

"Don't tell me," he said. "Don't tell me."

"The thumb is going to be all right."

"I'm not talking about your thumb. I'm talking about the job."

"It's just about over."

"Just about? Then it's not over?"

"Well, Pa, I guess it is."

"They fired you?"

"He didn't fire me."

"You mean you quit?"

"I didn't quit."

"What the hell do you mean?"

"I mean he sort of let me go. He was sorry to do it."

"You mean he kissed you good-by?"

"They fire you when you do something wrong, Pa. I just wasn't doing things exactly right. That's all there is to it."

"What is this? Why didn't he show you how to do it?"

"He did. But he didn't have much patience."

"Why not? You were new. Why didn't he?"

"How do I know? The same reason you don't."

"I don't understand this," he said. "I don't understand this."

"What's there to understand? I tried my best. I couldn't handle the knife as well as the others."

"What others?"

"The other men."

"But when did they start on this job?"

"I think some of them started today."

"Some of them?"

"Most of them," I said.

"You mean all of them. And they're going back tomorrow."

"Some of them."

"You mean all but you!"

"I guess so."

"What the hell is this? How could he see in one day that everyone could do it but you? How could he see it?"

"He looked. He was there every fifteen minutes."

"But what is it to cut meat off a bone? By Christ, you get it off with your teeth quick enough!"

"Well, it's not so easy. You've got to work fast and there's a kind of trick to it."

"Why didn't he show you the trick?"

"Well, he did. I don't know what happened. I was watching him and watching him. I saw where he started and where he finished. It's hard to explain. I couldn't remember what happened in between."

"It's the same when you talk to me!"

"Why do you get so upset about such a little thing?"

"A little thing? Is it a little thing that you can't hold a job for one day? Is it?"

"I thought it was. But it's getting bigger every minute. I don't think that job was worth holding."

"Don't you? The others thought it was."

"Let them hold it then. It's different for me. I wasn't meant to be a butcher. I didn't belong there."

"What were you meant for? Where do you belong?"

"It's something I have to find out. I'll look for another job and meanwhile I'll put in a couple of days a week on the wagon."

"Let me tell you something," he said. "If I see you walk in here with a watermelon I'll break it over your head! That job will be the ruin of you. I never heard anything like this in my life. One day on a job. One miserable day!"

"What difference does it make if it's one day or one week? They'd find out about me sooner or later. This way it saves time."

"What's in that package?"

"The boss gave me some meat for stew. It's beef."

"There it is. There it is in one word. It ends in stew. I can't believe it. All at once I remember myself at your age. I used to work all day in the mines and then study books half the night. I took hold of things and never let go!"

"Maybe that's your trouble, Pa."

"Get out!"

"And another thing: did you play the harmonica?"

"Get out before I lay my hands on you!"

He put his hand on the package of stew. I turned and went out. His curses followed me. Peggy was coming down the street. I stood on the sidewalk and watched the slow free swing of her body. It was like a hidden bell. Her face and eyes were aglow within the swimming black of her hair.

"Let's go up to Lincoln Park," I said. "I mean business."

"What's all the noise inside?" she said. "Is your father arguing with someone? Is something wrong?"

"Nothing at all. He's taking target practice. There'll be a big thump against the wall in a minute and then it'll be over."

The thump came. My father had thrown the stew against the wall.

"There it is," I said. "Now how about a movie?"

"I'm sorry, Paul. I don't think you understand things."

"Let's walk up to the Garden Theatre. We'll go by way of Lincoln Park. And then we'll come home by way of the park. Never mind the movie. Let's go right to the park. I'll play the harmonica and give you a ride on the swings. And then we'll get some ice cream."

"Edmund is taking me for a ride down to Perkins Beach. He bought a new car, Paul. A brand-new Chevrolet. It's pink and black."

Sudden jealousy like flame was leaping round inside me.

"Listen to your father," she said. "He's really wild."

"Why shouldn't he be? I lost my job."

"You lost your job? You mean your new job?"

"The brand-new one. It was red and white. Meat and bone mostly."

"How could you? How could you lose a job so fast?"

"It was easy. The boss said I was no good. Absolutely no good."

"He didn't?" she said, as though she suspected it all along.

"But he did."

"I'm sure he didn't mean it, Paul."

"Why did he say it then? And in front of everybody? Why did he call the office girls in to hear it? Why did he rip my apron off?"

"I can't believe it. What happened to your hand?"

"I cut myself. That wasn't so bad. The trouble is, I cut the man working next to me. But I swear it was an accident. You've got to believe that. He was leaning over to tie his shoe and I got him in the shoulder. And then the boss made a grab for my knife and I got him. On the side of the wrist. It was a shock. He's what they call a master butcher. He didn't spill a drop of his own blood in twenty years. He sent me home in a taxi."

A horn was blowing.

"Your new car's at the corner," I said. "Is he afraid to drive it in the alley? Tell him Danny Poulos is a big boy. He doesn't throw rocks at new things any more."

She went away from me as though going downhill.

I sat in the rocker on the porch. I was rocking and thinking about her with that boy. Surely she would whisper to him and kiss him. My father started to curse again. Now it was good to hear him. By the time he went to bed we were both at peace. I wished him sweet sleep.

Peace lasted as long as his sleep. First thing in the morning I called Sam Ross and then I made ready to go out on the watermelon wagon. My father sat looking away from me. His nose in profile hooked slightly and then pointed like a finger straight into hell. It was a dangerous time to tease him and yet that vengeful look was irresistible.

"I think I'll ask Sam for a raise," I said. "Sometimes people want half a watermelon and Sam tells me to do the cutting. Now that I've got more experience with a knife he should pay me more."

I jumped back as he turned the table over. He drove his hands into his pockets to keep from hitting me. He lunged into the bathroom and slammed the door so hard that plaster crumbled in the kitchen walls. I went to work and came home to find the table in the same place. He was lying on the bed and puffing his pipe.

"How about some supper?" I said. "Maybe we should have a buffet supper. Why should we let this table come between us?"

I kept talking while I put the kitchen in order. He said nothing. I went out to buy a loaf of bread and I stopped at the coffee house to tell Theodore about the situation at home.

"Your father's on edge, Paul," he said. "It's a hard time for him. A man works hard all his life and then one day they tell him he's finished. It's a bad thing. And then he doesn't see you getting started in the way he wants. But he'll be all right. Keep after him. Keep him busy with things."

I followed his advice. First of all I subscribed to eight magazines. My father watched for mail that never came and so now every week there would be new magazines for him. I was carried away by this idea of mail. Using his name, I wrote to inquire about correspondence courses in figure painting and vocabulary improvement and personality development. I called six travel agencies and told them to send folders with information about vacations in every corner of the world.

I played tricks to startle him out of black brooding moods. One windy night I removed the newspaper stuffing from three dining-room windows. Those rattling windows woke him at two in the morning. Late the next night I got out of bed to go to the bathroom. I turned the toilet handle straight up and went back to bed. I lay there listening to the water gurgling in the toilet and the deep harsh breathing of my father. Suddenly he snorted. Now there was only the big flooding noise of water as though from a burst pipe. With a cry he leaped out of bed and blundered into the kitchen where he ripped the chain off the kitchen light. He was cursing for half an hour. I had to bite the pillow to hold back laughter and a sudden wild cry of love for him in the night.

Next morning I was sipping coffee and watching him as he made preparations to go to the bathroom. He called it the high point of his day. He was wearing dungarees and brown slippers. He filled his pipe and put it beside the book of matches. He cut an orange in quarters and finished it in four bites. I poured coffee for him. Two sips were enough. His eyes flashed. He was just about to grab pipe and matches and lunge into the bathroom when I got up and slipped in ahead of him. I stayed in there. He was cursing and marching from room to room. I heard him in the bedroom. I slipped out of the bathroom. I closed the door and went out on the porch. Now he was in a dancing uproar. I started to play the harmonica. He came to the kitchen door and saw me sitting on the porch step. His mouth worked. No words came. He plunged into the bathroom and slammed the door.

I thought about him all day while selling watermelons. As always I was ashamed of myself for teasing him and yet I loved him even more because of it. I decided to buy a fine black hat for him on Saturday.

Next morning I filled his pipe and put it beside the matches. I sat waiting in the kitchen. There was no sound. I called out before going into his bedroom. He was lying in bed and staring at the cracks in the slant brown ceiling. His back and shoulders had stiffened in the night. Beads of sweat glistened on his brow. I stood over him for a moment and then moved away. I didn't want him to feel helpless.

"Is it your back again?" I said.

"Go away."

"If I go away, Pa, you'll be alone. So will I."

"Don't touch me."

He took a deep breath and tried to lift himself on his elbows. His eyes went hot with pain. Muscles bulged in his neck. All at once he made a turning lunge for the chair beside the bed and he fell with a sharp crack of bone on it. My heart stopped when I saw his thin white body hanging out of bed. I lifted him back. He closed his eyes against me. I turned him over and massaged him.

"It's like a knife," he said. "It's like a knife in my heart when I remember how strong I used to be. Life leads on to nothing."

I helped him into his dungarees. He got up and shuffled into the kitchen. He ate an orange and sipped coffee. Off he went to the bathroom. I moved his chair under the light. I knew that his hands would be unsteady and so I waited to shave him. He came out and sat down. I found myself pinning the dishcloth too tight around his neck. Without a word he jerked it down and off and dropped it on the floor. Apologizing, I pinned the cloth again and started to lather him with the brush. I lathered and lathered him. Something was telling me to stop and stop and yet I kept lathering and lathering. At last nothing was left but those eyes gone small with fury in a foam white and rich as his hair. He gave me a terrible kick in the shin. He went into the bathroom and stayed there until I left the house.

After work I stopped at the coffee house. An old woman was sitting with Theodore at the corner table. She was turning cards over one by one and telling his fortune. She kept sighing.

"Look at this," she said. "Let's see if there's a black queen. My, my. A change is in the wind. Very nice, Theodore, very nice. The coming year will be a good one. You're at the end of a poor cycle."

"It's a cycle that lasted sixty years, Ruth."

"A surprise is in store for you. Something you never counted on."

"You mean I'm going to die?"

"Patience, Theodore, patience," said Ruth. "Everything will turn out right if you have patience."

"What's going on?"

"What do you mean?"

"You used to have guts," said Theodore. "There was always enough trouble to put me on guard. You must be getting soft, Ruth. Maybe you better turn in your cards."

Theodore teased her awhile and then gave her a dollar and a glass of whiskey. He filled a glass for himself and lifted it to hers. Their eyes met and they smiled. In a moment they were laughing at each other.

I thought my father might like to have his fortune told. I asked Ruth if she would come around the corner with me.

"By all means," she said. "Lead the way. I won't be back on the South Side until the holidays."

On the way over I gave her two dollars and told her to make the fortune cheerful. My father was sitting on the porch. He sat up very straight when he saw us. I helped Ruth up the porch steps and led her into the kitchen. She sat at the table. She told me to wipe it clean and then she told me to pull down the window shade. I took a pint of whiskey out of the cupboard. I filled two glasses and we drank a toast. We had a second glass. That whiskey went to my head. I felt reckless and wonderful. I went out on the porch.

"She's waiting," I said. "She's all ready for you, Pa."

"Ready for me? Who is she?"

"She came to tell your fortune. At great expense. What a stroke of luck for us. What a privilege. Ruth is here with your truth."

"My what?"

"Your fortune, Pa. Come in, come in. The lights are low. If you only knew what she told Theodore. What thrills and shocks. What revelations. Theodore fainted. We called Doctor Fisher. Quick, Pa, quick. She's on a tight schedule."

"Jackass! Get her out of there."

"You're wasting time, Pa. She's due at the mayor's office. Be nice for a change. She walked all the way over in this heat."

"I told you to get her out of there."

"She came to see what's in store for you. She tells everything."

"Do I need her to tell me what's in store? I'll tell her. Tell her it's more of the same. Tell her it's sunshine and singing birds. Tell her it's moonlight and roses. Tell her it's love and wine and laughter. And tell her pretty soon I'll die and be in peace."

I went back inside. Ruth had the cards laid out and so I asked her to tell my fortune. She shuffled the cards and laid them out again. She told me I was in the midst of a seven-year cycle of good things. She spoke of a girl.

"A girl?" I said. "Does she have black hair? Plump? A little bowlegged? Does she live nearby? Tell the truth, Ruth."

"Yes, yes. She has dark hair all right. There's the queen of clubs. And she lives nearby."

"Will she be mine? My own darling Peggy? Wait, wait. Don't answer. I'll die if she won't. I can't even think about it. Wait then. How does it look to you? Is there a chance for me?"

"Jack of spades. Resistance."

"I know, I know. I wish you would put a spell on her. Wait then. Can you make a nose bleed in the distance?"

"Now what's this?" she said. "I see a stranger coming into your life. A stranger and not a stranger."

"Tell me more. Out with it, Ruth."

"From the east. The east, the east."

"Wait, wait. A stranger and not a stranger? From the east?"

"The east is right."

"In Pennsylvania? Is it possible, Ruth?"

"Very possible. Pennsylvania is east of Ohio."

"Then it must be Vandergrift. It's my father's first cousin. It's Michael! Is he coming here? Is he coming to see us?"

"It's very possible."

"This is remarkable. Wait then. Tell me something about jobs, Ruth. It's my big trouble right now."

"Don't worry about jobs. Everything will fall into place."

She drank another glass of whiskey. I helped her out the door and down the steps. She gave my father a cold squinting look.

"It's all over," I said. "Ruth told me everything will fall into place. She gave me her word."

"That place is the grave," he said.

9

Early Saturday afternoon I went downtown and bought a fine black hat for my father. It cost me twenty-five dollars. On the way home I saw a help-wanted sign in front of the Superior Forge & Steel Company. I thought it would be a wonderful surprise for my father if I came home with a new job as well as that new hat. I got off the bus and hurried into the front office of the plant.

Not one word did I say. A man with a smashed nose and eyes like ice caught my arm as though putting me under arrest. He studied me.

"My name is Rafferty," he said. "Do you want a job? I mean do you need a job? Tell the truth. Did you finish high school? You look all right to me, damn it. I'm fed up with these floaters. Can I count on you? Damn it, boy, I'll get you started in an hour here. I'll put you on the second shift. How about it? Bring your cake. Follow me."

Carrying the hatbox, I followed him into the plant.

First and last in that place was the pounding. It seemed that some tremendous hammers were dropping and dropping to pound everything into pieces. The pounding was off to our right and then it started in a distant corner of that black building. Rafferty guided me around the shipping dock. Beside and above it was a kind of conveyor. Swollen gray carcasses of steel were hanging from it on big hooks. One by one they loomed out of a hooded shed. Rafferty turned to take me down an aisle of ovens. Those ovens squatted like frogs and gaped at each other across the blackened floor. Tangled webs of pipe soared and were lost in the gloom. An overhead crane rumbled past blackened windows running the length of the building below the corrugated roof. One window was open on a square of blue sky. It was a world of sky. Pounding was everywhere. It packed the twilight air like thunder. Down in the distance a sudden door was opening on a flood of sunlight.

"On to the forging plant," Rafferty was saying. "Damn it."

He was turning into a darker jungle. I found myself going straight for the sunlight. I walked faster. I started to run. I ran down the aisle with that hatbox held high like a trophy. I ran out the door and past piles of rusting scrap-iron and over railroad tracks. A cry burst from me. I ran all the way around that long block of buildings and caught the next bus home.

My father was sitting on the porch. I put the box in his lap. He tore the paper off. When he saw the label he got up and carried the box into the kitchen. He took the lid off and lifted the hat out carefully as an egg. He turned it in his hands and felt along the edge of the brim with his thumb and forefinger.

"It's a good hat," he said.

"It's a Borsalino. It's imported from Italy."

He put the hat on. The brim slanted in a salute that curved back around the white of his hair and then swelled into a rich black perfect crown. He was watching the effect on me. For an instant there was a look so shy and forlorn in his eyes that I had to turn away from him.

"How the hell does it look?" he said, sensing my feeling.

"It looks nice, Pa."

Sunday we went out to spend the afternoon at Calvary Cemetery on Miles Avenue. We visited the graves of my brother and my mother. I had brought a bottle of soapy water and a pair of scissors. I trimmed the grass around their stones and then I washed the stones and cleaned the letters of their names. My heart was filled with such love that I wanted to embrace my father. I held his arm when he climbed into the bus. I sat close against him. He was wearing the new hat. Everyone looked at him. It seemed that everyone took pride in him.

After supper I went over to see Peggy. By then I was loaded with pity for myself and for my father. Surely Peggy would realize that I needed and deserved her love. Her mother told me that she had gone for a ride with Edmund Hatcher. I walked up to the coffee house and watched a pinochle game until midnight.

It was on the way home that I saw Peggy kissing Edmund in the car.

I stopped alongside the car. I put my head in the window to be sure of it. They were locked together in the dark. It seemed horrible to me. Fascinated, I put my head in farther as though expecting something better and worse to happen. Breathlessly I waited. There was nothing to do. I backed away and went home. All that night I lay awake listening for the last beat of my heart.

The next day there was shocking news about Peggy. I heard it in the morning and then I heard it after work from my father.

"She's getting married at the end of the summer," he said.

"I know all about it," I said. "I knew it all along."

"The boy's buying a ring for her. You lost the girl, too."

"I guess I never had her."

"I see things for myself."

"I don't mean it that way."

"Either you had the girl or you didn't."

"Well, I didn't."

"It was right there for you. You haven't got it in the clutch."

"That's got nothing to do with it."

"Nothing to do with it? By now I'd have the girl following me around with a mattress on her back!"

"A little louder. I don't think they can hear you in Lincoln Park."

"I'd have to padlock my bedroom door to keep her out at night!"

"You should be ashamed of yourself."

"The shame is on you, clown! Take a look at that other boy. He's like a wilted stalk of celery. I used to put boys like that in my pocket and forget about them. I never even asked their names. They say his nose bleeds. His nose would bleed when he heard my footsteps!"

"I thought it was settled between us. I really did."

"I know, I know. I was watching you. It was watermelon on her porch. It was music on the harmonica. It was blushing and sighs in the park. Did you seal it with a kiss?"

"It doesn't make sense. One night she's kissing me and the next thing I know she's going out with him. And now she's getting married. Well, I don't care about her now. I really don't. She hasn't got any respect. For herself or for me."

"Wake up! What the hell could she expect from you? A girl thinks of her future. That other boy's got a job in a bank. They're training him for a big job. He even goes to school at night. He does everything while you pick seeds out of watermelon and watch a horse's ass!"

"Wait then. Why should she be kissing me and whispering in my ear if she's going to marry him? Tell me that?"

"The girl is ready. Do you need a set of instructions? Get that pint of whiskey. It's not too late. Take her up to the park tonight. Wait, wait. Bring her here. I'll take a long walk. Sign your name."

"Do you listen to yourself when you talk?"

"Don't you know you're supposed to love your neighbor?"

"You're loose in your talk, Pa! And you're loud!"

"Haven't you got any blood in you? I'm diving into my grave and I still feel whips on my back! Ten years younger and I'd bring that girl down in her tracks! Right or wrong, fire the cannon! War is war!"

The arguments went on day after day in the slow tightening heat of summer. Rumor had it that Peggy was planning to be married in September. One desperate night after failing to see her again and again I drank two glasses of whiskey and put the pint in my back pocket. I took the harmonica and went out on the porch. I was waiting for that boy to bring Peggy home. New hope was bubbling up in me. I would give her a long drink of whiskey. I would whisper to her and devour her with kisses. I would tell her splendid things. Suddenly it would be a night of high triumph. I would sign my name with capital letters.

It was after midnight when I heard the car at the corner of the alley. Presently they were strolling toward me. I moved back into the darkest corner of the porch. They stopped right in front of the house. Peggy turned into his arms. They kissed. I thought it was heartless of her to turn to him right in front of my house. Now they were moving on. Trembling, I came down the steps. I watched them come together again under the trees. I threw that pint of whiskey high and far in the night.

One week later there was a party to celebrate the engagement of Peggy to Edmund. My father and I were invited. We stayed home. I was rocking on the porch when Peggy came looking for me. She showed me her diamond ring. She asked if I would play the harmonica for her guests. I was stunned. I looked at her.

"Will you, Paul?" she was saying. "We'd love to hear it."

"Are you serious?" I said. "Now it's time for me to ask you. Are you? What do you think I am? The entertainer at Lincoln Court?"

"My goodness," she said.

"What goodness is that? Tell me."

"What's the matter with you?"

"Nothing's the matter. You ought to be ashamed of yourself. You need a little music for your party and you thought of my harmonica. I'm sorry. I only play when I feel like playing!"

"Well, Paul, I'm sorry I came over. And I came special to get your father, too. I thought he'd enjoy himself."

"You were wrong. My father never enjoys himself."

"Don't act so silly."

"What do you know about my father? Are you going to tell me about my father? I'm telling you he never enjoys himself. He hasn't enjoyed one single thing in ten years. Why should he enjoy your little party? What is this? Is everybody supposed to be happy now?"

"Never mind, Paul, never mind. I'm sorry you feel like this."

"Like what?"

"The way you feel."

"It's the way my father feels. He's right. And you're not sorry. You're not sorry about anything. It's all words with you and not me. You don't know anything about me. I'm the one that's sorry. I'm sorry I feel anything at all for you!"

"What's the matter with you tonight?"

"Tomorrow I'll be all right. I'll go out on the watermelon wagon and lie all day in the sun. And I'll burn these feelings out of me. And then I won't feel anything at all. I'll be like you. And I'll tell you what. I'll make up a big song to celebrate it. Listen for it."

"Good night, Paul."

"And I'll be playing that same song on your wedding day. Only louder. I'll be sitting in the park across from St. Augustine's. Look for me. And maybe I'll be playing that night at your reception. And I'll be dancing to my own music. Because I'll be free! Forever!"

She went away. I sat rocking and rocking. I rocked myself close to tears. My father came out puffing his pipe.

"I'll be waiting to hear that song," he said.

"What song?"

"Your swan song. You were almost singing it right then. Now I'd like to sit in my chair awhile. Buy a chair of your own if your life is finished. We'll hold hands and rock together."

Everything was going wrong. My heart seemed to be melting away with the days of that summer. Now it was the delight of my life to start arguments with my father. First thing in the morning I played the harmonica. He woke with a curse. In the afternoon I came through the door playing to wake him from naps. He woke with a curse. All I talked about was my job on the watermelon wagon. I told him I would be known as the watermelon king.

One afternoon I brought home a police dog. That beautiful black dog had strayed into the alley. He was near full growth and yet eager as a puppy. He answered every whistle and seemed to be going in every direction at once. I saved him scraps of meat from supper. They were seasoned with hot pepper and he started to run in widening circles with his tongue hanging out. I gave him a piece of watermelon. Next day I took him out on the wagon. He put his head in my lap when I played the harmonica. He feasted his eyes on me. He gave sudden barks and wagged his curving black tail. Everything filled him with delight. I called him Prince and took him home.

He was thrilled. He was barking and sniffing and racing around the house. He bounded over chairs and under the table and in and out of every room. He growled my father out of the bedroom and then plunged into the cellar where the old smells of wine and cheese and mice made him so excited he was barking as though to burst into tears with all his luck.

"Where the hell did he come from?" said my father.

"Let me introduce a prince, Pa. The last of his line."

"Out he goes."

"Not so fast. I just bought him. One hundred dollars."

"Are you out of your mind?"

"It includes a whip to train him. He's a German Shepherd. A real champion. Look at those ears. He hears everything. Look at those eyes. He sees everything. Look at that nose. He smells everything. There's only one thing wrong. He's like me. He can't figure anything out."

"Get him out of here. I don't want a dog in this house."

"What a team you'll make. You can sit on the porch and bark at everybody. And then you can bark at each other."

My father was snarling and so Prince bounded up as to a brother and stood there with big soft paws on his chest. For a moment they were dancing around the kitchen. My father threw him aside.

"Grab him!"

"He'll be a watchdog for us, Pa."

"What's he going to watch?"

"The house and things."

"Is there anything worth stealing?"

"He'll warn you about things. He'll protect you."

"From what? All that's left is death!"

"Wait, Pa, wait. I've got it! We'll make a hunter out of him. We'll take him out at night on a big chain. And then we'll turn him loose. We'll get revenge, Pa!"

"Revenge?"

"Revenge on the neighbors! Revenge on the South Side for this smoke and dirt! Revenge on Cleveland! Revenge on life for smashing all our plans and everything!"

"By Christ, I really think you're losing your mind!"

He caught the dog and led him out. Prince was licking his hands and whimpering to win him over. It was no use. Prince ran around the house twice and then scratched at the door. He sat on the porch and when he heard a noise his black ears went up like wings. There was such innocence and beauty in him that my heart broke. Suddenly I was thinking of a lifetime of days and nights without my Peggy.

"And there's another thing," said my father. "I'm getting sick and tired of these letters. Do you understand?"

"What letters?"

"These letters offering me this and that. I don't want to paint pictures in my spare time. I don't want to repair television sets. I don't want to sharpen my wits or develop my muscles. I don't want to grow flowers on the window sills. And I don't want pills to get my juices flowing. My juices flowed away years ago."

"I didn't send for all of those. I guess they pass your name on. Wait a minute then. Maybe I shouldn't send this other letter. Be honest now. Do you feel rhumba lessons would be wasted on you?"

"Listen to me. Tomorrow morning you start looking for another job. I want you to look all day every day. Do you hear me? I mean it!"

Next morning I started out in search of work. It was the same old story. Those employers were interested in everything but the fact that I was ready and willing to work. Once again I wasted whole days filling out long applications. To put fun in it I made each one a little bit different. I kept changing my middle name. It was Randolph and Chester and Sebastian. It was Ferdinand and Sherman and Oliver. Within a week my grandmother had been born in Ireland, Greece, Russia, Turkey, Spain and Wales. I had hobbies like chess and badminton, whittling and fencing and archery. Those interviewers seemed troubled by the fact that I was single and so I said I was engaged and would be married in the fall.

In the end it went wrong. I was hired by John C. Cook of Central Chemicals Company. I didn't want that job. John C. Cook was excited about it. He was tapping his fingers and feet. He was telling me I would start on the night shift and he made the work sound like dancing in the dark until certain details lodged in my ears like pebbles. I sat there crossing my legs tighter and tighter as though to crack a walnut. I turned shy. He was even more eager to have me. It would be a grand opportunity for me. I would start by handling bags of potash.

"You'll handle two kinds," he said. "There's sulphate of potash and muriate of potash."

"Handle them? How much do they weigh?"

"Eighty pounds. Hold on a minute."

"I just let go."

"That's pretty funny," he said, slapping me on the knee. "I was going to say you don't handle the bags by yourself. You work in a team with another man. You swing the bags to a two-wheeler and then load them on trucks for shipment. You don't really lift the bags."

"You mean the other half of the team does the lifting?"

"You've got a good sense of humor, Paul. I like that.

What I'm saying is that you swing the bags. You're only moving about forty pounds at a time. There's a rhythm to it. Your body swings back and forth. It develops your muscles."

"Yes, sir."

"Let me tell you something in confidence," he said. "On a job like this we get a lot of drifters. I hired four men today and I'll bet they don't last a week. They'll work a few days for a paycheck and then quit. We can't find good steady men. There's a special program here. We're looking for pushers and foremen. From there you can move into the office or sales. How's that?"

"It seems all right."

"I'll set up an appointment for you with Doctor Fowler. Pass the physical and you start work on Monday night. Good luck, Paul."

I thanked him. It was mostly for saying my name. I went home and told my father about the job. I said they were putting me on a training program. Any change would have satisfied him. We ate together and then talked for a while.

"By the way," I said. "You can have all the potash you want."

"Good, good. Bring all you can carry."

After taking a nap I walked over to the coffee house. I sipped black coffee and watched a pinochle game. The gamblers were teasing Theodore. Marko was laughing in the corner. Nothing had changed.

I left there. I strolled up to Lincoln Park and sat on a bench. It was a night without stars. The leaves were whispering above me. I thought about Peggy. Suddenly I was overwhelmed by this need to tell and tell of the deep sweet love inside me. I went back to the alley. I slipped into her yard and moved quietly along the wall of the house. I sat down on the ground right under her upstairs bedroom window. The room was dark. I whispered her name. There was no answer. I felt the harmonica in my pocket. I took it out and turned it in my hands. I started to play. I played a song for Peggy. It was a song unknown to me. I played it again. A kind of peace was flooding through me.

The corner window opened. Her mother was there.

"Peggy's not home, Paul," she said.

"Thank you, Mrs. Haley."

"The music was nice."

"I didn't mean to wake you."

"I'm sorry about things, Paul."

"Good night, Mrs. Haley."

I went home. The screen door slammed behind me.

"Is that you?" said my father, from the bedroom.

His voice was like a slap in the face.

"Who is it?" he said.

I said nothing.

"Goddam it," he said. "Who's out there?"

"It's Michael!" I cried, hoarsely.

"Who?"

"Michael Christopher! Not your third cousin! Not your second cousin! It's your first cousin! I was sitting there, Carl, and I was wondering where it all started! And where it will end! And then I heard the song, Carl, I heard the song! I came all the way from Vandergrift! Come out, Carl! Come out wherever you are and give your first cousin a big kiss!"

My father turned over in bed to turn away from me. I started to laugh. I couldn't stop laughing. I sat there doubled up with laughter until tears came into my eyes.

10

Late Monday night I sat with nine colored men on the dock of the Central Chemicals Company. All around us were brown paper bags of potash in stacks of eight. Three trucks to be loaded were backed against the dock. I sat watching and listening to those men.

"Stopped in at Larry's Lounge Bar," one was saying. "No loungin' there. Walls painted red. Place smokes like a chimney. What dancin'. Like everybody's clothes on fire."

"This work's too heavy," said another. "I applied for a postman job. They'll be callin' me soon."

"How's it pay?"

"Side benefits. Sick pay and vacation. Pension. Other things, too. Look at Feef Carter. Feef's got a street he can't get through in the mornin'. Women call him in for cake and pie. Feef's cuttin' deep. He says the job changed his life. He went on like a light."

Two other men were talking off to my left.

"Hear you went up to the veteran hospital."

"My back ain't right, Dan."

"That so?"

"Can't go like before. Hate to see weekends come."

"What the doctor say?"

"Lay off the heavy stuff. Call that a doctor? Can't move and he tell me to hold still."

"Ask about that veteran pension?"

"Always do. Says you got to have a history of disorder."

"That was *you*."

"Said it all but my name. Got the longest history of disorder on Woodland Avenue."

Dan turned to me.

"You lost, boy?" he said.

"No. I think I belong here."

"You the only one," he said. "We all lost."

There was a whistling in the night. The foreman arrived. All eyes went to him. He was whistling and moving around as though stalking us. Pale blue eyes watched us from a round battered face. He was tapping the bulge of his belly in a loving way as though all his power had sagged there from the loosened swells of his chest and shoulders.

"Call me Greevy," he said, softly.

"Greevy," said a voice in the group, following orders.

"Greevy," said another.

"Greevy," said a third.

"Now what?" said the first.

"Now all together," said the second.

Several of them sang the name out.

"Thanks," said Greevy. "Call again some time."

"When's the best time?"

"When you feel like singing," said Greevy. "After you finish a good night's work. I see some new men here."

"Stamped and ready, Greevy. Wound up tight like toys."

"Let's have your O.K. slips from the doctor," said Greevy. "Any questions about the work?"

"This the place?"

"That's right," said Greevy. "You report on this dock."

"This the time?"

"Be ready for work at eleven," said Greevy.

"Where's the music?"

"What music?" said Greevy.

"Man said we'd be swingin' here."

"I'll furnish the music," said Greevy.

"Now what? Now what the hell? Now what the hell's with this potash? Now what the hell, Greevy, the hell with this potash?"

"They use potash to fertilize the soil," said Greevy. "Potash helps things grow."

"Don't need it. I'm the biggest thing on Scovill Avenue."

"You're about medium size around here," said Greevy. "And you're getting smaller every minute."

"When we get paid?"

"Once a week," said Greevy. "Friday."

"Be back Thursday."

"That's it," said Greevy. "Let's get to it."

"Now what? Now what the hell?"

Greevy divided us into five teams. My partner was over six feet tall. He loomed like a tree. Moving together, we started to swing those eighty-pound bags of potash. We loaded them eight high on a two-wheeler and took turns wheeling it to the trucks backed against the dock.

"What's your name?" he said.

"Paul, Paul."

"Mine's James, James."

"It's only one Paul."

"So I see. It's only one James. One's too much."

His laughter spilled forth rich and sweet as cream.

"Listen, baby," he said. "This job's a one-way ticket."

"How do you mean?"

"To the rupture wards. Bend your knees. Move when I move."

"All right."

"Slow down. Save yourself. Save me."

He was laughing again and bowing. Suddenly he was laughing uproariously as though there were no reason for it.

The high and low bags in those piles were hardest to handle. It was necessary to reach up and swing the top one down exactly right on the steel tongue of the two-wheeler. We had to be in control of that bag all through the lower half of the swing. Already there were sudden long pulls in the muscles of my arms and shoulders. The following bags were easier. We would swing them across and drop them before feeling their full dead weight. The last bag was hardest. We had to lean over and swing it up on top of the other seven.

Greevy had gone away.

After a while he returned. He was whistling to warn us. He stood there under a naked white bulb. His pale eyes were a little wild now as he looked around the dock. He was tapping his belly.

"Where's the guy in the yellow cap?" he said.

"Thrasher?"

"That's right," said Greevy. "Where's Thrasher?"

"What you want with Thrasher?"

"Where the hell is he?" said Greevy.

"Right here," said another, stepping forward and saluting.

"Not you," said Greevy. "Your partner. The yellow cap."

"He means Luther."

"What you want with Luther?"

Greevy hurried behind the dock where he found Luther smoking a cigarette. They came back talking.

"You know better than that," said Greevy.

"I do, Greevy."

"We break for a smoke at one and five. You know that."

"I do, Greevy."

"Well, what's the idea?"

"It's that rock, Greevy"

"What rock?"

"It's that sharp rock back there, Greevy. Had to sit on

that rock awhile. Been on a sharp rock thirty years. Born on one."

Greevy went away. He was whistling when he came back.

"Where's the guy in the sailor hat?" he said.

"Wheeler?"

"I mean the guy in the sailor hat," said Greevy.

"Sailed off, man. Went down with the ship."

"Wheeler was a sport, Greevy."

Greevy went behind the dock. He marched the smoker to work and then drifted away. Half an hour later he turned up. He was weaving.

"Where's the guy in the undershirt?" he said.

"Went to the doctor. Broke his hump."

Greevy kept everyone under control while losing control of himself. By now it was clear that he stopped whistling only to take a drink in some hidden place. He would go away whistling and then there would be silence. The men called out to him in the night.

"You gonna buy or be, Greevy?"

"Drown your sorrow! Drown mine!"

"Now what the hell is this, Greevy? Is it the whistlin' make you drink or the drinkin' make you whistle?"

"The man whistles clear and so he drinks," said Luther. "But he drinks to whistle clear. So he drinks to whistle clear so he drinks to whistle clear."

Those bags of potash were getting heavy for me. Each one seemed to weigh a pound more. I was doing less and less of the lifting. I tried to save my strength for the last bag. I would lean down to lift and all the muscles would stretch deep into my back. James had longer arms. He started to swing before I did and for an instant he was swinging me up along with the bag. He gave me mournful looks.

"You liftin' there?" he said.

"I think so."

"I don't know."

"Neither do I."

I was aching through the shoulders. My fingers dangled. James told me to go behind the dock and rest. I went back there. I sat on the big sharp rock with my arms hanging down. I felt dizzy. Suddenly I heard Greevy asking about me.

"Where's the little guy with the curly hair?"

"Had a cramp."

"Shipped out with the last load."

I sat on that rock trying to make myself disappear. Greevy came around the corner.

"How are you?" he said, bobbing and weaving.

"All right. Thank you."

"You're welcome, I'm sure. Let's go."

"Yes, sir."

"One man doesn't work and two won't work."

"I'm sorry. I had to rest a little."

"It's O.K. Get moving. But be careful."

As we came around one side of the dock my partner James went laughing around the other side. Greevy followed him. They came back talking.

"Too much turnover here," said James. "They come and go like it was a liquor store."

"You're right," said Greevy. "The company's got a labor problem. And you're part of it. So what?"

"Got a solution for you, Greevy. You buy eight baby gorillas. Train them up. No pay problem. You hang big bunches of bananas from the ceiling."

"I'll put it in the suggestion box," said Greevy.

I could hardly straighten up when we stopped to eat at three in the morning. I staggered into the locker room and sat down on a bench. One bite of my ham sandwich was enough. I was too tired to chew it. I leaned back and watched the other men. They were having a picnic in the dark. They ate chicken and pork chops. They ate ham and cheese sandwiches with lettuce and tomato and pickles. They lifted slabs of layer cake and cream pie. They washed everything down with milk or coffee. Finally they lit cigarettes and cigars. They stretched out on benches or melted away in corners. They puffed and dreamed and dozed.

Greevy was whistling in the doorway.

"Cork that man," someone said.

"Now what the hell?"

Greevy marched us to the dock. We started to swing those gigantic bags again. There was no breeze at all and the air was powdered through with white potash dust. I lost control of my muscles. Everything in me went soft as though I had been stuffed with cotton. The ends of those bags would slip through my fingers and hit the floor. James would be left holding his end up and waiting for me to lift again.

"You there?" he said.

"I'm here."

"Thought you left."

"I'm trying, James."

"You just pretendin'."

"I'm really trying my best."

"All right."

Greevy watched awhile and then he left. All work stopped. The men turned into statues in the dark. Faces were powdered with potash dust. I was watching the sky for traces of light. It was black and black. Morning would never come again. We were sinking to the bottom of the night.

There was whistling. Everyone stirred. Greevy reeled into our midst. His shirt ballooned at the waist. He was bobbing around. James and I were swinging a bag when he turned away. James returned that bag to the pile on the dock though it would have been just as easy to follow through on the swing and lay it on the two-wheeler.

"You a company man?" he said.

He was laughing and bowing again.

Greevy returned at dawn. It was my turn to push the two-wheeler to the truck. I stood on tiptoe to grip the swollen black handles. I gathered my remaining strength and snapped the two-wheeler back off the floor toward me. It was coming down on me. I caught it with my whole body and stood there dancing under it.

"O, God," I said, softly.

Greevy was interested. He was watching me as I started to push the two-wheeler. There was a slight ridge where the floor of the truck met the floor of the dock. I needed a good start to get over it. I closed my eyes and prayed for strength. I started to move faster. I was going well. Suddenly I heard a cry of warning. The truck was pulling away and that two-wheeler dropped clean through my hands and off the dock. I stood looking down at those spilled bags with my hands frozen in midair as though still holding the two-wheeler.

"O, God," I said.

"Never mind," said Greevy.

I turned to him.

"Put your hands in your pockets," he said. "Go back and sit down till I send for you."

I went back and sat on that sharp rock. Morning had come. Storm clouds moved across the sky like a herd of elephants. They massed over a bridge that swooped and soared in merry-go-round leaps across the Cuyahoga River. I fell asleep.

Greevy woke me.

"How you feeling?" he said.

"Not so bad now. Thank you."

"You're welcome, I'm sure. You look like you were turned every which way but loose."

"I guess you're going to fire me."

"Don't put it that way. This work's too heavy for you."

"I'll do better tomorrow."

"Maybe so. You'll either build up to the job or hurt yourself. I can't take a chance on you. You're a bad insurance risk for the company. I don't know what the hell's the matter with that Cook. Couldn't he see you're too small?"

"Is it all right if I take some potash?" I said.

"Help yourself. I'll mail you a check for the night."

"Do you know what? I was thinking about your job."

"Were you?"

"I wish I had a job like yours. I wish I had your job."

"Your ambition will carry you far," he said.

11

On the way home I stopped at the open market on West Twenty-Fifth Street and Lorain Avenue. I bought hot peppers and plum tomatoes for my father. I bought walnuts and poppy-seed cake. I went across the street to Gray's Drug Store and bought half a gallon of red wine. Candles were on sale and so I bought a golden one as big as a quart bottle.

My father was making coffee when I staggered into the kitchen. I showed him the groceries and the potash. I told him the bad news. He shuffled into the bedroom and closed the door against me.

"The coffee's ready," I said. "Come out and have your breakfast. Don't let a lost job spoil everything. Look what I brought you. It's a poppy-seed cake. And it's still warm."

There was no sound from the bedroom.

"Look what else I brought," I said. "You'll never guess. What a surprise. We'll have a celebration. And wait till you see this candle. What we need in this house is a light of gold. Things have been getting grayer and grayer since Nina left. Why should we live like spiders, Pa? Tell me why. From now on we'll eat and have our discussions by candlelight. Maybe we should dress for dinner. And then after dinner we'll have brandy and cigars. By candlelight. We'll go over the events of the day and make plans for tomorrow. I have this feeling we'll look better to each other by candlelight. We might even become friends, Pa. Tell me one thing. Is there any reason in the world why we should live like spiders?"

He came out and went into the bathroom.

"Now here's your horoscope in the *Plain Dealer,*" I said. "Are you listening? Pay attention. It says: 'Be audacious. Stimulating rays for mental work, developing new ideas, trying new fields. You are in a favorable position for personal, professional and business ventures. You should emphasize your fine imagination, foresight and keen judgment. There's no reason in the world for you to live like a spider.' Well, Pa, how's that sound?"

He was cursing his luck.

Next day I went back on the watermelon wagon and he wouldn't even look at me. He started to do the cooking. No longer could I eat that food. He loaded it with more and more hot pepper. Everything exploded in my mouth. One evening I sat there watching him prepare supper. He fried pork chops with cherry peppers. He put three more of those peppers in the salad. He boiled two potatoes and sliced them in a dish. He put olive oil in a frying pan and dropped in a handful of dried red devil peppers. He fried the peppers black and then poured everything over the potatoes. He sat down and took a deep breath.

"You forgot to set fire to the bread," I said.

Day after day he took terrible punishment. Sweat dripped off him. His mouth hung open and his dark eyes seemed to be melting away. In the middle of the night he would rush to the bathroom where he cursed fate and his scorched bowels. Afterward he went out to sit on the porch in the dead smoky air. Sometimes he rocked until dawn.

August had come. South wind brought clouds of soot and smoke from the mills. First thing in the morning I wiped all dirt away with a damp cloth. Next morning there would be dirt again as though some witch came in the night to sweep with a black broom over tables and chairs and window sills. All the curtains in the house had gone dark along the edges. It was like living black lace. Nina had promised to come twice a month to wash and iron the curtains. Finally Sophie Nowak offered to do it.

"Please mind your own business," my father told her. "I enjoy the curtains. I look at them and think of my daughter. I don't have much to think about these days. If you wash the curtains I wouldn't think of my daughter at all."

The long slow days of that August seemed to burn hope and delight out of everyone in the neighborhood. It was the worst month of the year. Two and three nights a week there was uproar in the Dew Drop Inn. Men came plunging through the door to fight in the street. Harsh cries went up like ugly birds. Presently the black and white police car came to scatter the crowd. One night the policemen jumped out of their car and someone jumped right in and drove it away.

There were bitter arguments in the coffee house. Seldom did the Greeks fight with their fists. They pounded the tables and insulted each other along with God. Each would listen and wait for the other to finish his speech. It went on to the point of danger and then as if by signal they turned and walked away big with triumph like kings. Most of them worked as painters of structural steel. They were related in various ways and those arguments would start about work or gambling and then shade into old family rivalries and foul play.

It was on one of those hot smoky nights that Rakowski smashed his furniture. He drank himself into a fury and staggered home to smash chairs and lamps and tables. Next morning he burst into tears when he saw the house in ruins. He cried and cried about it. He started to cry about his hatch-tender's job in the steel mill and then he cried because his daughter had run away ten years before with a Russian cabinetmaker. He cried about Poland and America and then because he had so much reason to cry.

A few nights later Florio drank too much wine. At three in the morning he was playing arias from the Italian operas on his phonograph. That music woke everyone in Lincoln Court. Someone called the police. Just before they came we heard this thrilling tenor voice lifted in the night. A sob was torn from the heart of that singer. Now his song was lifted again and given and lost in the giving like the soar of a fountain. Two policemen were pounding on the door.

That tenor was singing himself free of the despair that would soon fill my own heart. I had promised to free myself with a song. It was too late and too soon. For it was on the first day of September that Peggy Haley married Edmund Hatcher.

Three days before the wedding she came over to see me. All she talked about was her Edmund. He was brave and true. He was taking her away from the alley. I listened to her and then I kissed her hard on the mouth. Her body started to come alive. She pushed me away.

"Why did you do that?" I said.

"Do what?"

"Push me back like that."

"You shouldn't be kissing me, Paul."

"Why did you kiss me back?"

"I didn't. Besides, it's like a good-by."

"It didn't feel like a good-by."

"Well, it is."

"I just don't understand it," I said. "I really don't."

"Understand what?"

"You never gave me a chance. You were playing with me the whole time. What's wrong with me?"

"You're the one that's playing, Paul. You're playing through life. It was the same in school and everything."

"Was I playing with you? Didn't I tell you I loved you?"

"Are you talking about that night in Lincoln Park?"

"That's right."

"You're acting silly, Paul. Kissing doesn't mean that much."

"I guess it doesn't. But you're the only girl I ever kissed. And you're the only one I ever wanted to kiss."

"Kissing is like dreaming. It's like dreaming about love."

"Is it? When did you know you were dreaming?"

"I'm not sure."

"Did you know it then in the park?"

"Maybe I wasn't too sure right then. I do like you, Paul. I like you an awful lot."

"But you weren't too sure. How about Edmund? What if you wake up some morning after you're married and find out it was all a dream? You were dreaming about love. Like you did with me."

"That won't happen!"

"How do you know? You're talking to an expert on the subject. Ask anybody in Lincoln Court. Ask my father. He thinks I'm dreaming about life and everybody else is living. Maybe he's wrong. Maybe he's dreaming about me."

"Not so loud, Paul."

"And I'm beginning to dream about the neighbors, too. You should hear what they tell me. They stop me on the street. They give me all kinds of advice. They tell me I'm too old to work on a watermelon wagon. They tell me I should wake up. They tell me I'm too old to play the harmonica. I tell them I'm happy and they say no, no, no. Does it sound like I'm dreaming? What kind of life is this? I do my best and everybody thinks it's all wrong!"

"Not so loud. They'll hear you."

"What's the difference if they hear me? They know everything about me."

"I better go."

"Maybe you better. Why did you come over here in the first place? Wait, wait. Don't tell me. Let me guess. You want me to play the harmonica at your reception. Is that it?"

"No!"

"Why then? Do you want to be sure I'm suffering? Take a good look. And then go home. One of these days you won't be able to turn away so easy. You'll have to look things in the face. And I see that look in your eyes, too. Shame on you. Shame on you to be all excited like that just because I feel like I do!"

"I don't feel that way!" she said, bursting into tears. "I came over because my mother said you were at the house one night! Playing the harmonica for me!"

"And you're lying about how you feel!"

"I'm going, Paul!"

"And I'll tell you something else! From now on I'm never going to be in love with anybody! I mean it! Once is too much! This is the last time for me! From now on I'll be looking the other way!"

"Good night, Paul!"

"Good night and good-by!"

On the day of the wedding I was marching from room to room in the house. My father puffed his pipe and watched me. I went into the bathroom and slammed the door against his burning eyes. He called out that it was getting late.

"Late for what?" I said.

"Aren't you going to the wedding?"

"No, I'm not."

"Do you think you can hide from it?"

"What do you want me to do? Go over there and throw rice? Join the celebration? Play the harmonica for them?"

"It's what you promised. You talk a good game."

To spite him I rushed over to St. Augustine's Church. I was late and so I sat in the last pew near the door. The ceremony was ending. Father Murphy was saying those final precious words. A breathless silence followed. Edmund turned to kiss Peggy lightly on the mouth. So shy and innocent was it that my heart ached with sudden pity for them. I slipped out of the church. I went across the street to Lincoln Park.

The church doors opened. People streamed out and formed an aisle. Suddenly Peggy was there. Never had I seen such beauty. The sunlight of morning was caught by the shimmering white swirl of gown and veil. I had to turn away. All the love in my heart meant nothing. My darling Peggy was lost to me forever.

I went home. My father was reading a magazine on the porch. In that moment I resented his loneliness and blamed him for it. I was afraid to talk and so I hurried past him into the kitchen. He followed me. I wanted to cry out. It seemed he was in pursuit of me with loneliness. I went into the bathroom and locked the door.

"Is it over?" he said. "It couldn't happen and wouldn't happen. And now it happened. It's like death a little."

I said nothing.

"I knew you'd end up looking in the window," he said.

He was right again.

That night at the wedding reception I was looking through the window of the Polish National Home. Peggy danced with everyone. She was laughing and laughing. Her cheeks were like roses in the night of her hair. For a while I was hoping she would come to tell me that her heart was secretly broken. I was foolish. Never once did she think of me.

My final hope was that something would happen to ruin the wedding celebration. The best thing was to shoot myself through the heart and then fall across the doorway. I would die with my eyes open and that look would haunt Peggy the rest of her days. It would be a sensation in the newspapers. They would say I died for love. Afterward they would study my background and say I was unstable. I was thinking about it when trouble started in the hall. The butcher Kroger was serving at the bar and he scolded Rakowski for drinking so much.

"Why don't you stop awhile?" said Kroger.

"Are you paying for it?" said Rakowski.

"Drown yourself then," said Kroger.

A man beside Rakowski was muttering.

"What's that?" said Rakowski.

"Bartender's right," said the man.

"Listen, Greek," said Rakowski, putting his hand on the man.

"I'm no Greek."

"Russian!"

"I'm no Russian."

"What are you?"

"Polish."

"Liar!" said Rakowski.

He hit the man in the face. Kroger reached over to hit Rakowski on the side of the head. Rakowski turned and pulled him right over the bar. A crowd gathered around them. Everyone was pushing. Women were kicking and swinging their purses. Uproar spread through the hall like a wild new dance. The music stopped and started. The accordionist was playing "The Star-Spangled Banner." Someone hit him on the forehead with half a chicken.

Peggy and Edmund were being led through the front door by their families. Peggy was crying. I had moved away.

"They spoil everything," she said. "They just spoil everything."

"Never mind," said her mother. "Never mind them."

"It's all right," said Edmund.

"Your nose is bleeding," said his mother. "Did they hit you?"

"No, Ma, no," he said. "I'm all right."

"It's too much excitement for one day," said his mother. "You be sure to get your rest. Do you hear?"

"Please, Ma, please," he said.

There were kisses and tears. At last Peggy and Edmund were left alone on the sidewalk. They stood there in a helpless way. He took her hand. A piercing scream came from the hall.

"My God," said Peggy. "Let's get away from this place."

"I'll get the car," said Edmund.

He looked around as though lost.

"Well, what are you waiting for?" she said.

He went for the car.

Peggy was wiping her tears away when she saw me.

"Paul," she said, blushing. "Where were you?"

"I just came by," I said.

"Why didn't you come in? I was looking for you."

"I had some things to do."

"It's a fine thing," she said.

"What is?"

"You play the harmonica at everybody's wedding and you didn't even play one song for me."

"I played enough songs for you. It was a waste of time. From now on I'll play songs for myself."

"Where's your father?" she said. "We invited him."

"He's home."

"Is he all right? Is he feeling all right?"

"He's having trouble. With his bowels."

"Really, Paul, what's the matter with you?"

"Nothing's the matter with me."

"What a thing to say! And to a bride!"

"What was I supposed to say? He was dreaming of love and a star fell in his lap? My father's having his troubles. Just because you're a bride doesn't change his condition."

Edmund drove up. He got out of the car.

"Where were you, Paul?" he said. "I didn't see you. Why didn't you come in and have something to eat?"

We stood there. They looked abandoned. Once again my heart ached with pity for them.

"Congratulations," I said. "I want to wish you the best of everything. The very best. I mean it."

"Oh, Paul," she said. "You were always so sweet."

Finally she gathered up her white gown and slipped into the car. She scolded Edmund for closing the door before she had the dress safely inside. As they drove off she turned to give me a long look. She wanted to be sure she was leaving a broken heart.

I stood there. My heart felt like a prune. I wanted to lie down and die right on the sidewalk. I looked around. Fire from the steel mills leaped on the sky. The night was choked with smoke and dust. I thought of my father. It was good to know I could go home and have it out with him.

He was drinking wine in the kitchen. I started to slam dishes and cups around. All at once we were in an argument.

"I don't think she was the girl for you," he said.

"I guess not!"

"She's bowlegged, too."

"I know, I know! I wanted a bowlegged girl!"

"Besides, she was too fat for you."

"Too fat for what? I didn't have to carry her through life!"

"Maybe you'll wake up now."

"Wake up to what, Pa?"

"To the way things are!"

"That's why I'm dreaming!"

"By Christ, you act like a baby! Hold still a minute! I'll warm a bottle for you and powder your ass! And then I'll tuck you in and sing you a lullaby!"

We argued and argued. I came close to tears. He blamed me for everything gone wrong. I blamed him. He started to throw his glass at me and then saw there was wine in it. He drained it off. He gave me a scornful look and went into the bedroom.

After a while I made a pot of coffee. I took a cup of it out on the porch. I sat in the rocker and tried to play the harmonica. There was no music in me. I went back into the kitchen to make peace with my father. I invited him to come out and talk things over. I picked up the *Plain Dealer.*

"Listen to this, Pa," I said. "Here's your horoscope in the *Plain Dealer.* Are you listening? It says: 'In romance, personal and domestic affairs, be diplomatic. Some unexpected situations may develop. It's an opportune time for making needed improvements; also for travel and holding conferences.' Did you hear that? Maybe we should light the candle and have a conference. A peace conference."

I told him we should paint the house.

"I'll get that aluminum ladder from Theodore," I said. "He says I can lift it with one finger. We should start before the bad weather sets in. I was thinking we'd paint the house white and the windows black. The windows will match the curtains. And then we'll plaster the cracks in the walls. And how about wine, Pa? We should make some wine. Some strong wine. Some very strong wine to keep us going. Wait then. Maybe we should make whiskey instead. We'll get drunk every day. We won't care what's happening because we won't know."

I told him next year would be full of surprises for us.

"And another thing," I said. "I took your advice, Pa. I ordered a rocking chair with a cushion. We'll rock together. We'll hold hands and rock and make plans for revenge."

There was no sound from the bedroom.

"I might as well tell you the rest of it," I said. "Sam Ross was talking to me. He says he'll have to let me go unless I do better. It was a kind of a shock, Pa. And there's something else. Can you stand more bad news? Brace yourself. It's a terrible thing that I lost Peggy. I realize that. But I lost something worse. Are you listening? Two thousand years, Pa. I lost two thousand years of history."

Laughter was like sharp stones in me.

12

Sunday there was an advertisement in the *Plain Dealer* inviting a high-school graduate to apply for a personnel trainee job in the Clancy Wheel Works on the East Side. It sounded perfect. At last I would be doing the hiring. I told my father about it. Next morning I got up early and went over to that factory.

The job had been filled on Friday.

I rode the bus to the Public Square and strolled into the Terminal Tower. I called my father on the telephone. I put a handkerchief over the telephone and talked hard out of the corner of my mouth.

"Hello," he said.

"Paul Christopher?" I said.

"He's not home. Who is this?"

"J. T. Williams of Clancy Wheel. Who's this?"

"His father."

"Speak to Paul?"

"He's not home."

"This Paul's father?"

"Yes."

"Very good. Well, sir, your son just left here. I can't use him in personnel, sir, but I want that boy. I'm determined to make a place for him. I want him as an inspector on the wheel line. By heaven, sir, your son belongs on wheels!"

He hung up.

I wandered around the station. A train was hissing in. I hurried over to welcome the travelers. Afterward I bought a pint of red raspberries at the fruit stand and a loaf of raisin bread at Kaase's Bakery. Nearby was a photography booth and so I took four pictures of myself.

My father was eating eggs when I got home.

"I brought some dessert for you," I said. "Look here. A pint of red raspberries and a loaf of raisin bread."

Carefully he wiped the plate with his bread.

"I was too late for that job," I said. "They were running that ad in the paper since last Thursday. I'll go back with Sam until I find something better."

He looked up at me.

"I was thinking," he said. "I was thinking about your mother. And then I was thinking about our parents. And then I was thinking about their parents."

"Were you?"

"And their parents and their parents. My head was spinning. It's unbelievable. Where's the end of it? Where's the beginning of it?"

"Who knows?"

"How long ago did it start? Ten thousand years ago? Was it fifty thousand? A million? Think of the comings and goings during that time. Think of the accidental meetings. I was wondering about it. And then guess what happened."

"I don't know, Pa. But it's thrilling."

"You came through the door. With red raspberries in your hand and a loaf of cinnamon bread under your arm."

"It's raisin bread."

"And the harmonica in your back pocket. A minute later you were telling me you were going out to sell watermelons tomorrow. Now think a little. Does it all come down to you?"

"I see what you mean. Well, it sort of looks that way."

"Is that the way it looks?"

"But the story's not over, Pa. Don't forget that."

"Keep talking."

"I don't know what more to say. Wait then. I guess I did the right thing this morning. I thought it would be a good idea to take some pictures of myself. I was right. Just in case. Here they are, Pa. Four poses. One in profile."

He gazed at those pictures.

"Maybe you were right," he said. "Do you remember what you said the other night? Something about two thousand years of history lost? Maybe you were right."

I went out. I sat in Lincoln Park for a while and then I walked over to the coffee house. I told Theodore about the situation at home. He advised me to see John Zalewski who was councilman of the ward.

"It's time for a plum to fall," said Theodore.

"A plum?"

"One of those political jobs. All you do is show your face. Look at the job he got for old Saris. Saris works on that bridge over the Cuyahoga. He's what they call a bridge tender. He pushes a button to lift the bridge when a boat's coming through. The rest of the time he reads the newspapers."

"It sounds good."

"The trouble is, he's beginning to worry about everything in the world. And then there's Florio. Florio works in the liquor warehouse. He works about four hours a day if they watch him close. Lots of good jobs with the city, Paul. Maybe you'll work with the street department. They send you out in a truck and you drink coffee and straighten a few traffic signs. Maybe you'll be a park inspector. Or a building inspector. Tell John I sent you over."

To catch the next plum I hurried over to see the councilman. He lived across the street from Lincoln Park. His wife Lucy led me through the kitchen into the dining room. John Zalewski was talking on the telephone. He motioned me to a chair. He studied me and seemed to decide I was too small to be of much use. His brow was divided into two humps like that of an elephant and he had the flaring nostrils of a horse. Suddenly I was troubled. I wanted to leave there.

"Wait a minute," he was saying, on the telephone. "Let me get this right. You were exceeding the speed limit. You crashed a red light. You hit a parked car. And you had a drink or two before you started. Now you want me to fix a judge. Is that right? . . . I see. How about a promotion on your job, Nick? How about a scholarship at Western Reserve for the kid? Jesus Christ Almighty, wake up! Never mind. Why should you wake up after forty years? . . . All right, all right. I'll be there when your case comes up. Isn't your wife expecting? . . . Bring her with you. And don't send me cartons of cigarettes, Nick. It doesn't mean a thing to me."

He hung up. He watched me and waited. I told him Theodore had sent me over to see about a job.

"Are you a neighborhood kid?" he said.

"Yes, sir. Lincoln Court. My name is Paul Christopher."

"Christopher? Are you Carl's boy?"

"Yes, sir."

"Can you type?"

"No, sir."

"Can you drive a car? Got a license?"

"No, sir."

"Can you operate any machines?"

"No, sir."

"You should run for office."

He started to write a letter. He wrote slowly as a child and then he studied his work. He read it again and again.

"This letter will introduce you to Sam Curry," he said. "He's a personal friend of mine. He's a supervisor at the Dairy Carton Company. You don't want a city job."

"Yes, I do."

"No, you don't."

"Don't I?"

"What do you want with a city job? Private industry is the place for a young man. You want a job with a future. Sam Curry will see to it that you have every chance."

"I'll do my best."

"I'm counting on you. This is a personal recommendation. Just watch your step. Keep your mouth shut and keep your eyes and ears open. Sam Curry will be watching you. So will I."

I felt that everyone in the city would be watching me.

"How's Carl?" he said. "How's your father?"

"Well, he's having trouble with his stomach. And his back."

"Who isn't? Do you know I used to be his crane oiler in the steel mill? I think he was the best damn crane operator they ever had. He could lay that bucket down on a handful of ore. I saw him work sixteen-hour turns and he used to sing and shout up there all the time. Did he ever take you up there?"

"No, sir."

"He worked in this little cabin. The bucket hung on cables from a trolley, you know. The trolley rolled on tracks from the hatches to the pit. Remember the cars with gear-shift handles coming up from the floor? I guess you don't. Wait a minute. I think the sport cars got them now. Well, there were three handles in the operator's cabin. One of them was to move the crane from hatch to hatch. The others were to open and close the bucket. There were two other handles right on those handles. For moving the trolley. And then there were steam and brake pedals on the floor. I think that's about right. Well, the operator had to control everything. Why, your father was like a tiger up there. I'll never forget his gloves. They were black and shiny like metal from the way he gripped those handles."

"He's got a pair of those gloves at home."

"I sort of like your looks, Paul. Aren't you the one who's been working on that watermelon wagon?"

"Yes, sir."

"That's no job for a young man. This is what you want. A good start somewhere. I'll be watching your progress. Good luck and give my best to your father."

I shook hands with him and left. I went over to see Sam Curry at the Dairy Carton Company in Parma. He was chewing a cigar and blowing clouds of smoke. He kept glancing at me while reading the letter from John Zalewski. He finished the letter and gave me a challenging look.

"Well, all right then," he said. "I'll get you started as a feeder on the gluing machine. You'll work nights for a month and then you'll go on the day shift. You'll learn every phase of the operation. Plastic packaging is a relatively new field. The company's as new as the building here. You're getting in on the ground floor. No one's been here longer than a year. How's it strike you?"

"Very good, sir."

"All right then. I'll set up an appointment for you with the company doctor. You'll get a free physical examination and free life and hospitalization insurance. You'll share in the company profits. You'll get a production bonus at the end of the year. Come in tomorrow. I'll have your papers ready. By the way, how's John?"

"He said he's having trouble with his stomach."

"Who isn't these days? All right then."

That night I called Sam Ross and told him about the job. He wished me good luck and then reminded me that my job on the wagon would always be waiting. I felt uneasy. It seemed he was putting a spell on me.

Early next morning I went back to see the doctor in his basement office across the street from the plant. He pronounced me in excellent condition. I went to the company office and filled out applications. They took my picture and said they would have a badge ready for me when I started work that night. I went home and told my father that I was trying a new job. I told no one else and yet by noon on the following day everyone in the alley knew about it.

Just before eleven that night I arrived for work. I was carrying my lunch in a brown paper bag. A foreman called Schultz was waiting for me in front of the narrow black time clock. He shook my hand. He gave me the badge and I pinned it over my heart. I punched my new time card in on the clock. A hard little bell rang. I put the card in the black rack and followed Schultz to a kind of conveyor belt.

"This is where you work," he said. "You'll feed plastic milk cartons in this machine. The cartons will be glued up and then carried on this belt to the other end of the floor. They'll be stacked over there and made ready for shipment to the dairies. Take a handful of these cartons and lay them down in here like this. The machine will do the rest of the work. It'll take them in one at a time and pass them down to those two girls over there. Do you understand?"

"Yes, sir."

"Put your lunch down. Watch me a minute."

Without moving his feet he turned to grab a stack of the red milk cartons from the dolly beside him. He turned back and slapped them down into a cagelike iron mouth. Those cartons were drawn in fast with hard snapping noises. By the time Schultz turned back with the second stack the first one was nearly gone. He slapped in the second stack. One by one the cartons were drawn in from the bottom.

"It's easy to adjust yourself to this machine," he said. "It isn't too fast and it isn't too slowly. I mean slow. It never speeds up and never slows down. Listen to it. What do you hear?"

"A buzzing sound."

"The gluing machine is hungry," said Schultz. "Nothing's happening in there. Now listen when I put these cartons in."

It sounded again like repeated bulldog bites on bone. Schultz watched the whizzing cartons with bright blue eyes. His head jerked slightly when the last carton disappeared from the floor of the mouth. He turned and slapped in another stack of cartons. He was leaning over to watch. His mouth opened a little and his blue eyes went round as marbles. His head jerked again with the last carton.

"This machine really takes them in," he said. "Do you know I started on this gluing machine? That's right. It was my first job in this place. Now it's your job."

"Yes, sir."

"Did Mr. Curry tell you about the bonus here?"

"He mentioned it."

"The bonus depends on profit. Profit depends on production. Production depends on us and we depend on each other here. It's like a family arrangement in this place. Everyone is trying to do more than their share. Now we'll be counting on you to come through for us."

He shook my hand and went away.

The gluing machine was buzzing. I started to feed it. With both hands I gathered a stack of cartons from the dolly and slapped it down into the cagelike mouth. I turned for another stack. I turned back to find the mouth gaping empty at me. The machine was buzzing in an angry way. I slapped in the second stack of cartons. I started to move faster. Finally I unloaded that dolly and turned back in triumph. A man was pushing another loaded dolly into place for me. For a moment I stopped to look at it. Buzzing started in the machine. Surely everyone on the floor could hear it.

There was no time for me to watch what was happening. I turned to gather a stack of cartons. My glance went from the dolly to the black time clock on the wall. In the middle of my turn to the machine I saw a naked blazing bulb of light down in the distant corner of the plant. Above me were rows and rows of shining new light fixtures and so I began to wonder what lay under that lone bulb in the corner. I slapped the cartons into the mouth and glanced down at the beautiful red hair of the girl standing at the opposite end of the gluing machine. I slapped and turned. My eyes jumped from the clock to the bulb to the flaming hair of that girl.

All at once there were hard thudding noises in the middle of the belt. Milk cartons went flying in the air. I stood there in horror.

Schultz came rushing over to turn the machine off.

"Come with me," he said.

I thought he would fire me on the spot.

"Look at this," he said. "See the carton caught down here at the bottom? See where the edge is bent up? This one carton started all the trouble. You've got to be sure these cartons are straight at the edges when you slap them in. One bent edge will jam everything up in there. See how it happens? Now this machine doesn't make any mistakes."

"It doesn't?"

"Never. It's one thing you should understand. It's your mistake because the gluing machine's perfect. Think a minute. This machine is so perfect it stopped a carton that wasn't perfect."

"I understand."

"Now I don't mean it's your mistake. Sometimes these boys bend the cartons when they load them on the dolly. I'm only saying that we're to blame when this happens. It's not the machine."

Schultz pulled out the smashed cartons. He flipped the switch and the buzzing started. He slapped a stack of cartons into the mouth. His blue eyes went round and his head jerked when the last carton slipped away. He nodded to me and left.

The gluing machine jammed again just before lunch at

three in the morning. Schultz came over to pull out the smashed cartons. The lunch whistle sounded and he sent me to the locker room where I ate a bologna sandwich and a cherry pepper. I was very sleepy. I washed my face with cold water and went back to the machine at three-thirty.

For a while I was turning and slapping in a perfect rhythm with that machine. My glance jumped from the clock to the bulb to the hair of that girl. That hair was changing like fire. It was wild and free with dancing lights. I was falling in love. I was longing to touch that hair and kiss it. Suddenly I had this feeling that the gluing machine was biting a little faster. I stayed with it. I turned for a stack of cartons and slapped it into the mouth. I turned for another stack and slapped it. I turned and slapped. I slapped and turned. I turned and turned and turned. Tension was growing in me. I went over to drown it with a long drink of water.

Toward the end of the shift the gluing machine kept jamming up. It was startling to hear the solid thud of cartons and then to see them flying up crazy like flushed birds. I would turn the machine off as Schultz hurried over. He was becoming upset.

"You must be handling these cartons wrong," he said.

"I can't figure it out," I said.

"I figured it out for you a while ago."

"Yes, sir, I know."

"Now what? Are you going to climb on my shoulders? Stand back. How the hell can I see what I'm doing?"

Once he came over and there was such a mess that he had to pull out smashed cartons with pliers. He was cursing softly. He glanced at my badge and then took a good look. I was smiling in that picture. It seemed I was laughing at him and he could hear that laughter. He flipped the switch on the machine. He lifted a stack of cartons and looked down to see if the edges were straight. He looked sharply at me and then flung the stack down into the mouth. He leaned over to watch. At the same time he was watching me out of the corner of his eye. I was leaning and watching him. Our heads jerked together as the last carton disappeared. Satisfied, he went away.

It happened an hour before quitting time.

I was turning and turning. I was slapping and slapping. Nothing was left but the hair of that girl. The machine seemed to be biting faster and faster and faster. Now I was spinning to keep up with it. That hair was red and then alive with softer lights and then turning into a liquid crown of gold. Something was going wrong inside me. A cry wild as a bird was beating around my heart. Suddenly it came hot and hard against my throat. I was going to scream. Quick I leaned over to bend one corner of a carton in the middle of that whizzing stack. A moment later the gluing machine jammed and those cartons were flying in the air. I was breathing a sigh of relief when I heard Schultz cry out above the thudding of those cartons.

"Sonofabitch!" he said.

I turned.

"I saw that!" he cried, pointing at me.

"Saw what?" I said.

"Get out! You're fired! Don't say one word! Don't say one word or I'll smash your face!"

There was dead silence on the floor. Everyone had stopped work to look at me. I walked across the floor of that long building and started to go out. I was right under that lone white bulb when I heard quick heavy footsteps. Schultz was coming down on me. I stood frozen. Cursing, he ripped off my badge and tore my shirt. He dropped the badge on the floor and ground his shoe into it. He lifted his foot. There was a trace of a smile in that ruined picture. He kicked the badge away.

"Now get out," he said.

13

The worst had happened and yet there was a sense of peace in me as though I had scored a triumph. I was going my way lightly when I remembered my father. The thought of him was like a pillar of smoke in the lovely blue of morning. Suddenly I was troubled by my sense of peace. It occurred to me that I might be a little loose inside like Marko. The only difference seemed to be that Marko laughed for everyone to hear.

I stopped at Lemko's Bakery across the street from Lincoln Park. I bought Lemko's special lemon layer cake with butter cream frosting and lemon custard in the middle. I went home. My father was still in bed. I put the cake on the kitchen table. I washed my face and then I undressed and slipped into bed. I was thinking of the beautiful hair of that girl at the other end of the gluing machine. I was reaching over to touch that hair.

It was late in the afternoon when I woke. The house was quiet. A brown spider sat right above me on the ceiling. He seemed to be watching me from the edge of that long crack in the wallpaper. I named him Magellan and lay there watching him. Presently he went down the slant ceiling and disappeared behind the window shade. Sunlight had turned that shade into a golden map of delicate black scrawlings. There was no sound from the kitchen. In that moment I remembered the voice of my mother. I thought it was the most precious thing in life to come awake with the sound of a beloved voice.

I dressed and went into the kitchen. My father was sitting at the table. His hands were clasped around a cup of coffee. The lemon cake loomed before him. It was holding all the light in the kitchen. It looked like a living thing.

"Good afternoon, sir," I said. "We meet again. You'll notice I baked a fifty-pound cake to celebrate the occasion."

He said nothing.

"Don't say a word," I said. "Don't even move. I want you to be comfortable and happy. And please don't apologize. Don't apologize for the way you behaved yesterday. And the day before. And the day before. And the way you're behaving now. Don't waste time on apologies. I understand your nature. What's even harder, sir, I accept you."

He didn't move. It troubled me. Perhaps he had heard about that job. Nothing could be done. I put a pot of coffee on the stove and kept talking. I asked him what he wanted me to make for supper.

"How about some potatoes and cherry peppers fried in oil? How about a salad of tomatoes and hot peppers? We'll have some fish as a side dish. I'll go to the market and get that blue pike for you."

He shifted in the chair and looked up at me. We watched each other. It was strangely peaceful and yet it seemed that in a moment I would hear his heart pounding.

"The councilman was here," he said, softly.

I nodded and turned away.

"Don't turn away," he said. "Don't turn away."

"He got me this job."

"I heard about it."

"They fired me. I deserved it."

"His friend called him with the news. John was so upset he threw up his breakfast. He's been telling everybody on the street about you. He came here to drag you out of bed. I stopped him. Not only that. I told him not to talk so loud. The words popped out of my mouth. It's like I didn't want him to wake you from your beauty sleep."

"I don't know what to say, Pa."

"Don't you? You mean you've run out of words for yourself? It's worse than I thought."

"I mean I can't explain what happened."

"What's to become of you? What's to become of you?"

"I was working and working and it was all right. And then the next thing I knew he was throwing me out. I did a wrong thing. Something happened inside me."

"What happened?"

"I don't know, Pa. But there's another thing. I didn't

even care about it until I thought of you. And even now I don't really care about it. I was trying, Pa. It was for you."

"For me? How hard did you try? How long will this go on?"

"I'll be all right. Wait and see. I'll find a place where I belong. I don't want that job. I don't like that kind of work."

"That has nothing to do with it."

"Why should I spend time doing something I don't like?"

"What time did you spend? You didn't even finish one night."

"But I would've spent more time there. It was a steady job. It would've been day after day and month after month. And then years."

"But it's the same with any job," he said, trying to control himself. "It's the same with life. Don't you understand? You don't stop living because you don't like it."

"Something happened inside me. It's like I was being choked up. It's like dying. I'll be all right when I find what I like."

"What do you like? Besides playing the harmonica?"

"I'm not sure, Pa. I'll find out."

"When will you understand that work is work and not play? When will you understand this? They pay for work and not to make you happy. You can't do as you please in life. It's only people with money who do as they please. And they do nothing."

"But I'm free. I'm free to look for what I want."

"Listen to me. This freedom is nothing. It's worse than nothing. In fact, it's a slavery. You give in to yourself. You give in and give in. But one of these days there'll be no choice for you. There'll be no way out for you. Life will come down on you like a lion and there'll be nothing left in you to meet it."

"I'm saving something, Pa."

"What are you saving?"

"A terrible scream."

His eyes closed. I watched him. He looked old and weary. Suddenly I was remembering the days of his strength.

"Listen then," he said, softly. "I want you to find a place to stay. I think it's the best thing."

"A place to stay? What do you mean, Pa?"

"I mean what I say."

"But what are you saying? What place is there for me to find? My place is here with you."

"But I don't want you here."

"But this is my home, Pa."

"It's a home for no one."

"It's not true. It's a home as long as we're together."

"Then it's a home no longer. Don't you understand? You make me so nervous I can't eat or sleep right. I want peace. I want peace."

"Why do you get nervous? Is it these jobs? Is that it?"

"Some of the neighbors stopped here this morning. They were asking about you and John Zalewski. A few of them were laughing. And then one of the women looked at me like she was going to cry."

"Why do you listen to people? I walk away when they talk about you. It's all words to me. I belong with you and not with them."

He pounded the table with his fist and then swept the cup against the wall. He stood up. His eyes flashed and his mouth was working even before words came.

"Is this where you belong?" he said. "Do you think you belong here with me?"

"What is this? Of course I belong here."

"You're wrong! Do you hear me? You're wrong! Put it in your head! I say you'll have to find a place for yourself! You don't belong here any more!"

"Wait, Pa."

"The waiting is over!"

"Listen a minute. Tell me what you want me to do. I'll do anything you say. Just tell me."

"But I just told you," he said. "I want you to get your things and leave this house. I want you out of here tonight!"

"You don't know what you're saying. You're all upset. How can you send me away? How can you even think of such a thing?"

"I know exactly what I'm saying," he said, softly now. "I don't want you here with me. Do you understand?"

"But I'll be with you whether I'm living here or not. There's no one but you, Pa. I have to see you and be with you."

"I called your sister," he said, nodding. "She hasn't got any room for you right now. But it's better. It's better for you."

"This is like a dream. Wait a little. Wait till tomorrow."

"No. It's tonight."

"But winter is coming and everything. Who'll take care of you in the mornings?"

"Worry about yourself."

"I'll tell you what, Pa. I'll quit the job with Sam. I'll go out every day looking for another job. I'll find something good. And I'll stick to it. I swear it. I can do it. I'll force myself. How's that?"

"It's for you and not for me."

"Tell me what you really want then. Tell me right out, Pa. Do I talk too much? Is that it?"

"I don't want to argue."

"But it's nothing to argue about!"

"Look at me," he said. "Take a good look. I'm tired. I go to sleep tired and wake up tired. Don't you understand? I'm tired of life itself. I used to wonder about things. I used to wonder why certain things happened in life. I used to drink and swear. I used to smash things and ask questions. Now I don't even care why. It's enough that certain things happen. It's too much. All I want now is to lie down and die in peace."

He shuffled out to the porch.

I sat there watching him through the door. He lit his pipe. He smoked and rocked. It was quiet in the alley. Suddenly it seemed that the neighbors had heard everything and were waiting for me to leave the house. I was deeply ashamed for myself and for my father.

I went into his bedroom. I pulled the old black suitcase out of the closet and took it into my room. I wiped it inside and out with a damp cloth. No one ever used that bag. I packed some socks and shirts and underwear. I closed the bag and started to tighten one of the frayed straps. The end of it came away like paper in my hand. I cut the rest of that strap away from the bottom of the bag. I started to tighten the other strap. It came away in my hand. I sat down on the bed and looked at it. It seemed a cruel thing that the second strap broke. I cut the rest away. Finally I lifted the bag and it dropped back to the floor. The handle of it was left in my hand.

After a while I pushed that bag into the kitchen. I was going to call Sam Ross and then I changed my mind. He lived too far from Lincoln Court. I called Theodore and explained the situation. Laughing, he told me to come right over. He would set up a cot for me in his rooms behind the coffee house. His laughter relieved me a little.

My father had stopped rocking. Smoke curled up from his pipe. I took a deep breath and pushed the suitcase through the screen door. I stood on the porch and waited. He was staring straight ahead.

"Well, Pa, I guess I'm about ready," I said. "I'm going over to the coffee house. I'll stay with Theodore."

He nodded.

"You know the telephone number," I said. "Be sure to call if there's anything you want. Call any time. But I'll be here tomorrow."

I wanted to tease and turn him to me.

"I've got this feeling," I said. "I've got this feeling you're breaking some law. I'll have to put this in the hands of my lawyer."

He was watching a flag of fire in the sky. I lifted the suitcase to my shoulder. All at once my heart seemed to shrink away.

"Well, Pa, I'm ready. I guess you know something. I guess you know I'd never send you away from me. And you're the only one who could send me away from here."

"Good night," he said, softly.

I went over to the coffee house and stood outside until Theodore saw me. He waved me around into the yard. He was waiting for me at the back door that led into his kitchen. He greeted me with an open smile. Theodore was sensitive about his lost front teeth and so I was grateful for that smile. His head was bobbing as though to music.

"Come in, Paul, come in," he said. "Put the bag down."

"Thank you, Theodore."

"Don't worry about things. It happens every day."

"Does it?"

"Sure it does. My old man used to throw me out when he couldn't think of anything else to do. He'd go fishing a few days and then he'd get tired of it and send for me. Leave your things. There's a poker game out front. I'll make the rent tonight. Come out there. I'll fix you a cup of camomile. It'll settle your stomach. When the game breaks up we'll go down on Bolivar Road for some lamb and rice."

I followed him into the dining room. A door led from

there into the coffee house. Six men were sitting around the big table beside the counter. Marko sat alone near the door. Theodore warned him to watch out for the police.

"Hello, Paul," said Regas. "Say, I heard that speech."

"What speech?" I said.

"The councilman made a speech about you. In the Dew Drop Inn. He spelled out your name, too."

"I heard that speech," said Poulos. "I felt proud. It always makes me proud when a South Side kid stands out like that."

"What language was he talking at the end there?" said Regas.

"I think it was Polish or something," said Poulos.

"A man really chokes on that Polish language."

"Why don't you mind your own business?" said Theodore.

"Why don't you mind yours?" said Regas. "Why don't you put a fan in this place and blow the smoke out? And why don't you serve a sandwich or spring for a round of drinks? You'll end up with all the money in the game. And take off your mask."

Talk died away. The gamblers concentrated on the stud poker. I sipped camomile tea and watched the game. Theodore kept reaching in to take a quarter or a half-dollar out of the pot. He reached in while the last card was being dealt. The players were so absorbed in the last round of cards that they paid little attention to him.

Suddenly the front door flew open. Everyone cried out and jumped as though the table had burst into flame. There was wild grabbing for the money. Two policemen had come plunging down big as elephants.

"Stand back!" they cried. "Hold still!"

Marko got up and came toward Theodore. He was pointing to indicate that two policemen had arrived on the scene. He gestured again to let Theodore know that the police car was parked across the street.

"Good work," said Theodore. "Now's the time to laugh, Marko."

One of the policemen scooped the remaining poker money into a pile. He took a paper bag off the counter and put the money in it. Afterward he leaned back against the wall. He was watching us in a vaguely troubled way as though we were in a car going out of control in the distance. Small dark eyes were packed like seeds into his craggy head. The handle of his gun swelled in a single fat curve out of his holster. The other policeman was leaning on the counter. He rested his head on his hand and gazed at Theodore as at some strange rare animal.

"Good evening, Mr. Ampazis," he said, in a lilting voice.

"What's the meaning of this, Nick?" said Theodore. "I just came in here to make a phone call."

"Is that a fact?" said Nick, gravely, turning to the other men.

"Do you want the fact?" said Theodore. "I was calling you boys. I was going to report these men. They're gambling. Now I don't allow gambling here. These men are breaking the law. I hate to do it. Take them away, Nick."

"What's the delay, Theodore?" said Regas. "Give Nick the ten dollars you put aside for him and let's get on with the game."

"Did Mr. Ampazis say I'd take a ten-dollar bribe?" said Nick.

"If you couldn't get twenty," said Regas.

"There you are, Joe," said Nick, to his companion. "Two Greeks and you got a civil war. . . . Wait a minute. Do I smell whiskey? Are you bootlegging again, Mr. Ampazis?"

"Let's have another drink and go home," said Poulos.

"You don't even know your way home," said Nick. "Didn't I see you in a coffee house on Bolivar the other night?"

"I haven't been downtown in a month," said Poulos.

"You're going down tonight," said Nick. "Call the wagon, Joe."

The other policeman went out.

"I told you about this," said Nick. "I told you to keep the money off the table. You never learn."

"The boy wasn't playing," said Theodore.

"He shouldn't be here," said Nick. "What's your name?"

"Paul Christopher, sir."

"Where do you live?"

"Well, I'm living here for the time being."

"Are you one of these smart guys?"

"It's the truth," said Theodore. "He'll be staying with me a few nights."

"A night in the tank'll teach him a lesson," said Nick.

Presently the black and white police wagon pulled up in front of the coffee house. Marko stood up. He gestured to let Theodore know that an even bigger police car had arrived. We marched out. Marko watched us. He started to laugh.

"Take the clown, too," said Nick. "He was spotting."

The other policeman took Marko by the arm. Marko was laughing harder. He almost fell backward as he climbed into the police wagon. He was doubled up with laughter as the wagon took us away.

Down at the police station they took Theodore aside and put the rest of us into an iron room lined with open dark cells. Those Greeks came apart and went off to find private places.

I sat alone in my cell. Nearby Marko was laughing softly. A sharp disinfectant was burning in the still air and yet it failed to overcome thick sour smells of sweat and whiskey and old clothes. Iron doors were closing and closing in the night. Each door seemed to close more exactly. I heard the casual clink of keys and then a door opened lightly to close in some high hidden corner of that building. There was the liquid shuffle of shoe leather down some corridor. A moment of silence followed. Keys were clinking. A door opened to close.

I was thinking of my father when they brought Theodore back.

"You can go, Paul," he said. "Here's the key to the place."

"What about you? And the others?"

"We'll be out on bond in a couple of hours. I called my lawyer. Don't worry. They'll fine us a few dollars and that's the end of it. Good night, Paul."

A policeman let me out with a warning to be careful in the future. I went down the stairs and out into the night. I walked from Payne Avenue across to Euclid Avenue. I was walking toward the Public Square. I was walking faster and faster. I started to run. I ran all the way to the Terminal Tower. I went down into the train station and called my father. The telephone was ringing and ringing.

"Hello!" he cried, howling a little.

I thought my heart would burst with love for him.

"Hello, hello!" he said.

"Hello, Pa!" I said, breathlessly.

"What is it? What happened?"

"I'm free, Pa!"

"Free?"

"They let me go!"

"Who let you go? What happened?"

"I was in jail, Pa!"

"Jail?"

"I was watching a poker game. In the coffee house. The police came. They called the wagon. They took us down and put us in the tank. Theodore's still there. With Regas and Poulos. And the others. Marko's there. They let me go."

There was a moment of silence.

"Do you know what time it is?" he said.

"No, Pa."

"It's after one!"

"Is it? Is it that late? Are you all right? Is everything all right over there? I was thinking about you and so I thought I'd better call. Do you need anything special tomorrow?"

There was silence.

"By the way, Pa, did you put that cake in the refrigerator? It'll spoil if you leave it out. There's custard in the middle."

He hung up.

14

Early every morning I stopped at Lemko's Bakery to buy a cinnamon or poppy-seed roll for my father. I went over to have breakfast with him before going out on the watermelon wagon. He sat there puffing his pipe and listening to my foolish words. I felt like a child come to play before him with new toys. Sometimes he rested his head on his hand and gazed at me across the table. Never had he looked at me like that. I talked and talked to hold his eyes on me. I was bubbling over with new hopes and plans.

One morning I was thinking about buying a car in the spring and taking him on a trip into every corner of America. We would spend a year on the road. We would follow the sun from sea to sea. He was listening and watching me. Presently he was looking over my shoulder at some crack in the kitchen wall. In the end he was looking into the light of morning.

During the day I called him on the telephone from different parts of the city. Often he picked up the receiver and said nothing. To stir anger in him I said nothing. We waited and waited. I began to breathe harder. He hung up. I called right back. He picked up the receiver and waited. The pride in him filled my heart with delight.

"Well, sir, I don't agree with you," I said. "But you've got a right to think what you please. How's everything at the house?"

"How was it a couple of hours ago?"

"Things are developing. The plaster's falling at a steady rate. I saw encouraging signs on the floor in the bathroom. And then there's that crack in my bedroom ceiling. It's working all the way across into the corner. It's like a lightning bolt hit. It's kind of exciting to go in that room. By the way, Pa, what do you want for supper? Have you got a craving for something? I'm near a Big Deal store and I'll bring anything you want."

"There's nothing."

"Sam and I saw Father Murphy this morning. We gave him a watermelon. Guess what he said? He said watermelon was like a big answer to a big question. He said big questions call for big answers. And then he asked me a couple of pretty big questions. He asked why he never sees me in church. And then he was asking about you."

"Tell him I was asking about him."

"All right."

"Tell him I was asking about church."

"All right."

"Tell him I was asking about God."

After work I stopped at the house to make supper for him. He ate whatever I put in front of him. Later he walked over to Lincoln Park where he sat on a bench and puffed his pipe. The children played around him. They tumbled in the grass and chased each other under the dying leaves of the maples and sycamores. The light of day faded. At last the children went away and the park was quiet. My father walked home. He took a bath and rinsed out his underclothes. For hours then he sat sipping wine and smoking his pipe on the porch.

I called to tell Nina about him. She promised to come and spend a few days with him as soon as she had the chance.

"And there's something else," I told her. "I've been thinking. I think it's about time you had a baby, Nina."

"Do you?"

"I really do. You could call him Carl and bring him over here on the weekends. It would be a good thing for us."

"Would it?"

"Of course it would. What's the matter with you? Just think of it. He's got a grandfather and an uncle waiting for him. I'll tell you what. I'll start putting some money aside for him. I'll help you with the bills and all. How's that?"

"Do you have any idea what you're talking about?"

"You don't understand. You don't understand how Pa feels about things. Listen a minute. He's pretty sure there's no hope for me. And no hope for you. And no hope for Andy. But how could he be sure about a baby? Let me talk to Andy. I'll explain it to him."

She hung up.

Saturday noon I left Sam Ross and went over to clean the house. I mopped the floors and dusted the furniture and washed the towels and sheets. I took the curtains across the street to Sophie Nowak. She washed and ironed them and then she came over to hang them for us. My father stayed in the bathroom while she was in the house.

"It's safe to come out, Carl," she said. "I'm leaving now."

I took a bus to the market on West Twenty-fifth Street. I bought round steak and lamb chops and mustard greens. I bought small baskets of plum tomatoes and hot green finger peppers. I bought walnuts and figs and a gallon of red wine. I filled two shopping bags.

The next two buses were crowded and so I let them pass. I waited awhile and then found myself walking across the Abbey Bridge. Halfway across the bridge my hands and arms began to ache. I put the bags down. There were red furrows in my palms from the handles of those bags. I saw the nuts and wine and peppers. I lifted the bags and started off again. At the end of the Abbey Bridge I put them down. I sat on the grass under the ramp of the new innerbelt freeway bridge. I was aching all over and yet the pain of it was so good that I laughed. I carried those bags home.

I broiled the lamb chops with parsley and garlic. I boiled the mustard greens and then put olive oil and lemon juice on them. I cut the tomatoes into olive oil seasoned with origan and garlic and dried hot pepper. After supper we sat on the porch.

It was harder than ever to get my father talking. He nodded and mumbled in reply to me. My words were like pennies falling into a long black well. I played the harmonica when I could think of nothing more to say. He enjoyed the music. He sat there puffing his pipe and listening with his eyes closed. I played well. I climbed and climbed with words only to reach the place where songs begin.

One night while strolling in Lincoln Park I realized that his birthday was coming. I decided to have a party for him. Excited, I went over to tell Theodore about it.

"I know he wants me in the house," I said. "I can feel it. But he's stubborn, Theodore. He won't even talk about it. And he's been different since I left. The only time he eats is when I'm there. He doesn't listen to the radio and he doesn't even read the newspapers. This party might be just the thing to bring us together again. Winter is coming and everything."

In the following two weeks I saved most of my pay. I bought beer and wine and whiskey. Two days before the party I bought ham and salami and hot sausage. I stored everything in the soft-drink cooler in the coffee house. After that I went downtown to buy a television set.

A salesman showed me a polished box with a twenty-one-inch screen. I walked around it. He turned it on for me. Girls were dancing in candy-cane tights. Their legs were like whipped cream. I watched them. The salesman changed the station. Cowboys on horseback came down on us in a thundering smoke. I watched them. The salesman changed the station. A beautiful young lady was telling a young man that she was no longer in love with him. She went on to say that she doubted whether she had ever really loved him in the first place. I watched her. The salesman changed the station. Those dancing girls were getting reckless. The salesman turned the set off. Quick he turned it on again. Those girls were flinging their legs and arms in every direction. Off went the set. I turned to that wizard of a salesman. His hand was on the knob of the set. I watched him and waited. He was giving me a cool masterful look.

"I think you've had as much as you can stand," he said, smiling.

"I'll take the set," I said. "I'll put fifty dollars down."

"Do you have a steady job?" he said. "Will you be able to pay the two-hundred-dollar balance?"

"I've got a job. I sell watermelons in the summer."

"Is that so? What about this winter?"

"Well, I'll work in the market selling fruit and vegetables."

"All right. When would you like to have it?"

"Saturday morning. I'd like to have it delivered to a coffee house. I'll give you the address."

"Saturday morning then. Do you know what that means?"

"No, sir."

"Saturday night the girls dance just for you."

I went back to the South Side. I spread word that my father was going to be sixty-six years old on Saturday and that I was giving a surprise party to celebrate it. The neighbors promised to come. I called Nina from the coffee house and told her about it. Last of all I sat down to write a letter to my father.

DEAR PA,

Happy birthday to you and many more of the same!

I'm sure this coming year will be a good one for you and for me. I've been taking notes and making plans for the past twenty years. Now it's time for action.

First I'll put the house in order. I'll do some painting before the bad weather sets in. Theodore has this aluminum ladder I can lift with one finger. It's right here in the corner beside the table where I'm writing this letter. I'll borrow it to paint the outside of the house and then I'll plaster the cracks in the walls and paint the kitchen and bathroom.

Now the next thing for me is a good job. I was talking to Theodore about this problem. He says I'm finding out what I don't want to do in life and it's the only way to find out what I really want to do. One of his friends told him to tell me I should be a male secretary. I should learn typing and shorthand and then pretty soon I'd be making seven or eight thousand dollars a year. The name of this friend is John Pappas and he's a lawyer with an office in the Union Commerce Building downtown. John Pappas is the one who gets Theodore out of jail. He's only thirty-one years old and he's been married three times. Theodore says there's something wrong somewhere.

As soon as I'm settled in a good job I'll get married.

I've been looking and looking for a girl ever since Peggy went away. Naturally I hope to have quite a few children. I'll call my first son Carl after you and I'll call my first daughter Jenny after Ma.

Well, Pa, sometimes I wish we were the same age. I wouldn't mind being sixty-six years old. I'd be drawing a pension and I wouldn't have to worry about jobs. Better yet I could sit on the porch with you and smoke a pipe and we'd understand each other perfectly. I'd be good company for you. Maybe I'll buy a pipe and quit this job and just pretend for a few years.

Happy birthday!

Your loving son,
PAUL

Right after work on the day of the party I warned my father that the neighbors were coming to eat and drink and celebrate his birthday. He surprised me by saying nothing. He took a bath and shaved. He was dressed and waiting by the time I brought the last of the refreshments from the coffee house.

He was sitting at the kitchen table. I glanced at him and then I looked again. His eyes were clear and steady above the swoop of his nose. The bones in his face bulged white to give him that wild starved look. His mouth was trembling a little as though with the singing rush of strength inside him. He wore his shiny blue serge suit and a white shirt that had gone yellow at the collar tips and cuffs. He wore a black knit tie. He looked at me and then down at his scuffed shoes.

"I'll shine them for you," I said.

I brought the polish and brush. Kneeling, I started to shine his shoes. It was good to kneel before him. I put my hand around the back of his thin ankle while brushing each shoe. The strength in him seemed to leap through me and yet there was an ache in my heart reminding me of the absence of that strength in recent days.

I went across the street to call Sophie Nowak. She came back with me to help prepare the food. We sliced ham and salami and then we fried the hot sausage. We set the table with dishes of pickles and olives and tomatoes and hot peppers. In the center of the table was the big sponge cake baked by Lemko. There were six white candles across the top and six across the bottom.

The first guest to arrive was Lefty Riley. He was wearing a brown cap with a chunk missing from the peak. Bowing, he swept that cap off as though he had brought it for that purpose. He glanced at the loaded table and then shyly looked away. I introduced him to my father. They sat and talked like old friends. Presently the neighbors were coming in to fill the house with talk and laughter. They drank toasts to my father. They lingered to talk with him about baseball and politics and the economic recession. He seemed to be drinking in every word spoken to him. Now and again a strange sweet smile would light his face. So warm and alert was he that the neighbors began to interrupt each other in their eagerness to tell him things. At one point Rakowski was saying that he had disowned his daughter while Florio was shouting that life had no meaning and that God was a great comedian.

"We haven't got a chance here!" said Florio. "Not a chance!"

I went over to the coffee house to get the television set. Poulos helped me lift it into his painting truck. Theodore told Marko to watch the coffee house. He brought a tray of *baclava* and rode back to the house with Poulos and me. There were cries of delight as we struggled through the door with that television set. We staggered through the kitchen and set it down in the middle of the living room. Everyone milled around it. My father nodded to me.

"It's beautiful," said Sophie. "Paul is such a good boy."

"It's about time you had one of these," said Kroger.

"You'll see what's going on," said Florio. "And then you'll say to hell with it."

"This calls for a drink," said Rakowski.

"With a beer chaser," said Lefty.

There was a movement to the table for food and drink. Glasses of beer and whiskey were lifted lights of gold all through the house. The men raised their voices. No one listened and so they talked louder. There were bursts of laughter like reckless invitations from the women. A gray cloud of cigar and cigarette smoke hung from room to room like a ghostly fish dissolving against the ceilings. Sam Ross walked in. He smiled and his golden tooth flashed.

"Where's the watermelons?" said Poulos.

"This calls for a drink," said Rakowski.

"With a beer, God bless us," said Lefty.

My father kept glancing toward the door. I realized that he was watching for Nina. I stepped out on the porch. After a while I went over to the coffee house and called her on the telephone.

"But Andy isn't home yet," she said.

"Leave a note for him," I said. "Come right over."

"He wanted to come, too."

"Where is he?"

"He went to work out at a gym."

"At this hour?"

"He must be on his way home by now."

"Pa's been waiting for you. He really has. Don't disappoint him, Nina. Not tonight."

"All right, Paul. I'll be right over."

I went back to wait for her on the porch. Half an hour later she came in a taxicab. She kissed me. She had a white package tied with a green ribbon. We went inside. My father smiled when she leaned over to kiss him. She burst into tears and gave him the package. He turned it around in his hands. He fumbled with it and finally got it open.

"It's an electric razor," said Kroger. "A Schick."

"This calls for a drink," said Rakowski.

"Not a chance," Florio was saying.

"How about some music?" said Lefty.

He cleared a space in the kitchen and set a chair for me. I played the harmonica. There were calls for a jig and a polka and a tarantella. When it was time to light the candles on the cake I played happy birthday to my father. Nina put the lights out. I was playing and watching my father as he stood over the dancing golden lights of those candles. It seemed his face had been cut from white stone and then washed clean by his foaming hair. He blew out the candles. Everyone was singing to him in the dark.

After that the neighbors started to leave. They shook hands with my father and wished him well. Rakowski and Florio invited him to supper. Lefty invited him to go fishing at Gordon Park. My father thanked them. Sophie Nowak was the last to go. My father took her hand. He thanked her for preparing and serving the food. She was like a young girl afraid of her longing to be kissed.

Nina offered to help me put the house in order. She kept talking about Andy and so I told her to go along home. She called a taxi.

"Now I want you both for dinner," she said. "I want you to come next Sunday. Will you promise, Pa?"

"All right," he said.

"We should see more of each other," she said. "Andy likes you."

"Andy?" he said.

"He really does," she said. "He always asks about you."

"Andy who?" he said, gravely.

"Please, Pa," she said. "Don't be like that. . . . Here's the cab. I'll call you tomorrow. Good night and happy birthday."

I moved chairs back into place. I swept the kitchen and emptied the ash trays. I washed the dishes and glasses. My father sat there smoking his pipe. He looked exhausted and yet peaceful.

There was wine left in one of the bottles. I filled two

glasses and took one to him. We drank a toast. Suddenly a mouse was nibbling in the kitchen wall. The fragrance of all that food had put daring in him. We listened to the nibbling. Plaster crumbled softly.

"There isn't much for him," said my father.

Delicate scratching started in another corner of the wall. Plaster crumbled again. Both mice were still.

"I better be going," I said. I didn't want to embarrass him.

"It was a good party," he said.

"Don't worry about these bottles. I'll get rid of them tomorrow."

"Come for dinner. If you want to."

"Maybe we should have some spaghetti. I think there's hot sausage left. We'll put it in the sauce."

"Good."

"And then we can try the new television."

"All right."

"Well, Pa, I guess I'll be going. Good night."

"Good night then."

I turned away.

"Paul," he said, softly.

My heart stopped when he said that.

"Yes, Pa?" I said, turning to him.

He was watching me.

"What is it, Pa?"

"Well, I was thinking," he said.

"About what?"

"I was wondering here."

"Go right ahead, Pa. You can say whatever you want."

A sudden dancing light was in his eyes.

"Theodore," he said.

"Theodore? You mean Theodore Ampazis?"

"Yes."

"What about him?"

"Has he really got that aluminum ladder?"

"He really has," I said.

I was going to tell him about that ladder and then I saw the look on his face. He was teasing me. Laughter came into his eyes. For a long moment we were watching each other. It was good between us and so I turned to leave him before something happened.

15

It was in the dark of morning that I woke to the deep free snoring of Theodore in the next room. I thought of my father. I was longing to be with him and to see again the light of laughter in his eyes. Quietly I washed and dressed. I started to go out the kitchen door and then I remembered the aluminum ladder. I went into the coffee house. Laughing softly, I lifted that ladder with one finger. I put my arm through it and carried it out.

Morning light was climbing in the east over a coil of cloud like the fallen tower of night. I carried the ladder through Lincoln Park. Sparrows gossiped among the brown leaves. I turned the corner of the alley and glanced down at our porch. I was disappointed. I had hoped that my father would be watching for me.

I carried the ladder up the porch steps. I called out a

good morning and walked into the kitchen. I waited and listened. There was no sound in the house. The door of the bedroom was closed. I tapped it. I listened and tapped again.

"It's me, Pa," I said, opening the door.

The curtains were stirring in the breeze.

All else was still.

My father was on the floor at the foot of the bed. He looked broken. He was dressed the same as when I left him. I was gazing down at him. I started to watch for movement. I was watching until I realized that I was not really watching at all.

Carefully I stood the ladder against the wall. I went down on my knees to lift my father. Breathing deeply, I put my arms under him. It took everything in me to lift him and to stand with him. I held him in my arms. I was holding him and feeling a new strength that finally made him one with me.

I put him on the bed. I buttoned the coat of his suit and folded his hands over it. I looked at him. After a moment I went to the bathroom for a washcloth. I wiped his face and combed his hair. I kissed him on the mouth and then drew the sheet over his face.

I went across the street to tell Sophie Nowak. A kind of excitement was gathering in me. Sophie was getting ready for church. Her hat looked like a black war helmet. A red flower soared from it.

"Good morning, Paul," she said.

"Good morning, Sophie."

I waited a moment.

"Sophie, I think my father is dead."

She looked sharply at me. She turned very pale. She ran out of the house. I ran after her. I was wondering why we were running. I followed her up the porch steps. She hurried through the kitchen into the bedroom. She closed the door against me.

When she came out she put her arms around me. She kissed me hard on the mouth. She was hugging me so tightly that we swayed. I wanted to stay in her arms. As though sensing it she stood away from me. She filled a glass with whiskey and gave it to me. It went flaming down into me. It was delicious.

I sat at the kitchen table while Sophie made telephone calls. I was beginning to feel a little reckless. Sophie called Doctor Fisher and the police and Nina. Doctor Fisher lived right around the corner in Grant Court. He came in a few minutes. He was carrying his black bag as though he had forgotten all about it. The shrunken dissatisfied look of him stirred laughter in me. I wanted to tell him that we meant to call him in earlier on the case. I had to bite my lip against crazy laughter. I pointed to the bedroom. I got up to follow him and he told me to wait.

The police ambulance like the paddy wagon pulled up in front of the house. A policeman hurried in. I told him the doctor was with my father. He went back to the porch and called something to the other policeman. Doctor Fisher came out of the bedroom. He saw the ambulance and waited for the policemen to come inside.

"Probably a coronary," he said. "Three or four hours ago. You didn't hear anything, Paul? Where was your father?"

"He was on the floor," I said. "I didn't spend the night here. We had a birthday party for him and then I went over to spend the night at the coffee house. I've been staying there awhile."

"The police will take your father, Paul."

"Take him where?"

"Well, the authorities have to satisfy themselves as to the cause of death. Your father had bursitis and maybe some arthritis, Paul, but he wasn't under my care for anything really serious. Call the funeral director after while and he'll make the necessary arrangements."

One of the policemen asked me questions about my father. He was writing the information down. Sophie interrupted him.

"I'm putting the coffee on, Paul," she said. "And I'll make some eggs for you."

"I don't think so. Thank you, Sophie."

"How would you like them?" she said, stolidly.

I looked at her. She was determined.

"Fried in butter," I said. "With some dried hot pepper."

"Where's the pepper?"

"The pepper's in that jar on the stove. Put the pepper in first, Sophie. It fries black and flavors the butter."

The policeman waited. It seemed he was waiting for further word about the pepper and eggs. Finally he asked me a few more questions and then he nodded to his companion. Doctor Fisher leaned over to say he was leaving me pills to help me rest. The policemen went into the bedroom with a wheeled stretcher. They closed the door. Doctor Fisher expressed his sympathy and squeezed my hand as though to keep hold of me. Presently the bedroom door opened. The policemen were carrying my father through it. A blanket covered him. The policemen went stiffly through the kitchen and out the screen door. Doctor Fisher followed them. Sophie put the eggs in front of me. The yolks were fried solid. I hated the look of those eggs. I was running my hand around the edge of that dish. Suddenly I wanted to throw it against the wall.

After eating a little I sipped coffee and watched for Nina. I was anxious to see her. There was a kind of curiosity dark as greed in me. I was beginning to be ashamed of it when she arrived with Andy. I got up and went to her. We hugged and kissed each other.

"Oh, Paul," she was saying. "Oh, Paul."

She was sobbing and trembling in my arms. I nodded to Andy. His wild curly hair had gone gray at the temples. He looked like a lost child. I reached over to shake his hand.

Everyone sat down. Sophie served coffee. I put whiskey in mine. Nina wanted to know what happened after she left the house.

"Tell me everything," she said. "Everything."

"Everything? Pa's dead."

"What happened after I left here?"

"I cleaned up the house. I put things in order. We had a glass of wine and then we talked about having dinner together today."

"How did he look? How was he acting?"

"He looked tired. But he looked nice, too. Sort of smiling."

"Smiling? About what?"

"It was about a ladder. I kept talking about painting the house and borrowing this aluminum ladder from Theodore Ampazis. I mentioned it several times."

"Then what?"

"Well, I wrote him this letter for his birthday. I told him about the ladder again. Last night I was leaving and he called me back. He started to say something and then he changed his mind. Maybe he was going to tell me to come home. But I don't think so. Well, he didn't know what to say and so he ended up asking me if Theodore really had that aluminum ladder. He was teasing me."

"And then what happened?"

"That's all."

"She means today," said Andy.

"You see what happened," I said.

"She means all of it," said Andy.

"I woke up early. I decided to bring the ladder to the house. I was really going to start painting this week. And there he was."

"Where?" said Nina, softly. "Where was he?"

"On the floor. At the foot of the bed. Doctor Fisher said he died about three hours ago. It's a couple of hours after I left him. Probably a heart attack. I remember him saying he didn't know why his heart went on beating."

"How did he look?" said Nina.

"The same as last night. All dressed."

"I mean how did he look exactly?"

"Do you want to know?"

"Of course I want to know. What's the matter with you, Paul? You ought to be ashamed of yourself."

"I'll tell you how he looked. He looked like he was all used up and God threw him aside."

"Paul!"

"It's the truth. Do you want me to lie about it? It's what went through my mind when you asked me and I remembered him on the floor."

"He was all alone," she said. "O my God.'

She burst into tears. She stood up and started for his bedroom. Abruptly she turned and went into my room.

By and by the neighbors were coming to pay their respects. Some of those men strode into the kitchen as though taking command to save a ruined ship. Their eyes flashed. The word of death had filled them with strange power. Others came in a gentle whispering way. They were moving around me like men balancing on ropes. They shook my hand. It was a kind of dark precious welcome. They lingered to talk with me if I wished. They were careful not to intrude. The women came with bread and cake and pots of hot coffee. Their eyes were big with tenderness and sudden love for me. They touched my hands and my face. Several of them kissed me. Afterward they went in to comfort Nina.

I thought of Peggy. I wanted Peggy to come and see me at the heart of things. I was watching for her while listening to the talk that started in the house. I tried to follow every conversation. The words were like stones in the air.

"He looked good last night," said Mrs. Rakowski.

"Yes, he did," said Kroger.

"Didn't he look all right to you?" she said.

"I thought so," he said.

"You never know," she said. "You never know."

"Do you remember his wife?" he said.

"Jenny," she said, quickly. "Her name was Jenny."

"That's right," he said. "A beautiful woman."

"Yes, she was."

After a moment Mrs. Rakowski turned to Sophie.

"How did Carl look to you last night?" she said.

"He looked good," said Sophie. "Carl always looked good."

Florio was talking in the dining room.

"Carl got married," he was saying. "He was so happy he sent for his brother in Italy. Paul is called after this brother. That man was always smiling. He agreed with everything you said. He used to put his arm through yours when he met you in the street. But he couldn't get settled here. It's like he was in a trance or something."

"I think I remember him," said Rakowski.

"You should," said Florio. "Remember the day Carl brought him to the mill? He was going to break him in as a crane oiler. Paul was supposed to grease and oil the crane. It was only twenty minutes of work every two hours. He came in wearing a black cap like Carl. Carl bought him that cap to make him happy. Don't you remember that day?"

"I don't think so," said Rakowski. "Maybe I was working nights."

"Carl took him out on the wing of the crane. Now those wings are high. They went down to grease the winch at the end of that wing. Paul was nervous up there. He was holding Carl so tight he forgot to hold the grease bucket. He dropped it. It almost hit the fireman on the head. I think it would have killed him."

"Who was that fireman?" said Rakowski.

"I don't remember," said Florio.

"Was it Joe Zawada?" said Rakowski.

"Maybe it was Joe Zawada," said Florio. "I don't know. What difference does it make? The bucket didn't hit him."

"I was trying to place when it was."

"Well, Carl took Paul inside the crane. He showed him where to oil and where the grease cups were. And then he went down in his cabin to start up the crane. Paul was sitting upstairs and then all of a sudden the trolley was rumbling through there. And then the steam was hissing and the big cables were snapping and everything like it was going to explode. Paul went home. Carl said he remembered to take his lunch. It was his first and last day in the crane."

"What happened to him?"

"He was here another few months. He used to wear that black cap everywhere. Carl sent him back to the old country. He was herding sheep in the mountains and then one night they found him dead up there. It's like he fell asleep. They were saying in the village it must have been the moonlight. And he was wearing that black cap."

I wanted to see Sam Ross. I called and told him what happened. After a while he arrived in a taxicab. He was wearing a rumpled black suit and a black leather bowtie. It was good to see the dead black of those clothes. He came to me and squeezed my hand between his own. His eyes brimmed with tears.

"I'm sorry, Paul," he said. "I can't tell you."

"Thank you, Sam."

"How are you feeling?"

"I'm not sure. I really don't know."

"That's the way of it."

"I thought it would be worse. I guess it will be."

"Don't be afraid."

"I do feel kind of strong. Like someone's going to hit me."

He nodded and sat down beside me. We listened to the talk in the house. His eyes were troubled. He leaned close to me. He started to say something and then changed his mind.

"What is it, Sam?"

"It's nothing important. Do you know what? I was thinking yesterday about the winter and all. I was thinking of buying a little truck and going around with fruits and vegetables. I used to have a truck in the winters. I'll do it if you come with me, Paul."

"Were you going to say something else?"

"It was your father," he said. "I remembered something."

"Tell me, Sam."

"I was sitting here. I remember one day I was waiting for him to come from work. I was sitting right here at the kitchen table."

"What happened?"

"Your mother, God bless her, was roasting red peppers on the stove. There was a knock at the door. Your father came in. I was wondering why he was knocking at his own door. He was wearing that black cap. I don't even think he saw me, Paul. He took the cap off and he was looking at your mother. And then he said hello to her. It's like he met her the day before."

Time wore on. There was no wind to stir the clean white curtains. Smoke from cigars and cigarettes filled the room. Hour on slow hour the neighbors drifted in and out of the house. Late in the afternoon John Zalewksi stopped in for a few minutes. I stood up to shake his hand. He took my hand and didn't let go of it.

"I'm sorry about that job," I said.

"Forget that job," he said.

"It was all my fault."

"The hell with that job. And Curry, too. I'm sick of listening to him about it. I came here to pay my respects."

"Yes, sir."

"I liked your father. Let me know if there's anything I can do. Let me know if you want me to act as pallbearer. I'd like to do it."

"Thank you."

He squeezed my hand and went out.

Toward evening the talk faltered and then ceased in the house. The day would last forever and yet it seemed there was nothing more to be said in the world. The women started to put the house in order. They washed the dishes and swept the floors. They were asking me sharp little questions as though to keep hold of me.

"Paul," said Mrs. Rakowski. "What should I do with this ham?"

"Please put it in the refrigerator."

"It should be wrapped first. Is there any wax paper here?"

"The wax paper's in the cupboard. See it there?"

This talk seemed an excellent thing to me. I was eager and precise. I answered one question and waited for another.

"Where does this chair go, Paul?" said Mrs. Kroger.

"That chair goes in the cellar," I said. "I brought it up last night for the party."

"It's funny. Were these legs cut short or something?"

"My father cut that chair down for my mother. She used to sit in that chair when she changed us. Or when she nursed us."

"Is that so?"

"Yes, Mrs. Kroger."

I wanted to say more about that chair. She sensed it and waited. We were looking at each other.

"That chair can be left up here for the time being," I said.

"All right, Paul."

She was still looking at me.

"I might want to sit in that chair," I said.

"All right, Paul."

At last the house was in order. Talk ceased again. Outside it was dark. The silence seemed to be growing around us like the night. Suddenly the house was split by a sob from

Nina in the bedroom. There were hushed words from Andy and Sophie. Nina was crying softly.

Now the neighbors made ready to leave. The women looked around with a kind of satisfaction. There was nothing more to be done. The men came to me and offered to act as pallbearers. Afterward they moved closer to their women. They were filled with care and watchfulness. Presently they went away. I had the strange feeling that I would hear sudden big shouts of yes and yes in the night.

Andy led Nina into the kitchen. Sophie followed them. Nina burst into tears again. She hugged me and kissed me. She wanted me to come and stay with her. She begged me to do it.

"I'll stay here," I said.

"But I want you with me," she said.

"Please, Nina. I want to be here."

"Don't worry about the arrangements," said Andy.

"What arrangements?" I said.

"The funeral arrangements," he said. "I called the funeral director. He'll take care of everything. We'll be here early tomorrow morning. Try to get some rest, Paul."

They left.

Sophie put a pot of coffee on the stove. She sat at the table across from me. We looked at each other. My father was right when he said her face was like a cauliflower. As though for the first time I remembered that her husband was dead and that her married son had moved to Los Angeles. I was anxious to know about them. I started to ask questions. It pleased Sophie to talk about her family. I listened for every word and yet I could grasp the meaning of none of it. A moment later there would be another question popping out of my mouth. I leaned forward to listen to her. It seemed I was sinking through black still water lit here and there by the gleaming senseless details of her life.

She served the coffee.

"Will you eat something, Paul?"

"I've been nibbling all day. Maybe I'll have some whiskey."

"I'll get it for you. Are you staying here tonight?"

"Yes."

"I'll spend the night with you if it's all right."

"It's very nice of you."

She filled a glass with whiskey. I swallowed it in one gulp. It was raw and blinding. It was so good that I filled the glass again.

"That's enough," she said, sharply, taking the bottle.

I drained the second glass. It seemed to burn me clean inside. I sipped coffee. I was feeling reckless again.

"I'll get some things," she said. "I'll be back in a minute."

"Good. I'll fix my bed for you."

That whiskey went to my head. Everything was spinning around me by the time Sophie returned. I told her I was going out for a walk. She took my hand.

"Are you all right, Paul? Tell me now."

"I'm all right."

"Are you sure?"

"Yes, Sophie."

"I'll wait up for you."

I kissed her and went out.

Night seemed to be waiting for me. I walked out of Lincoln Court. The mills below were like the smoking ruins of an entire city. I walked faster and faster. Terrible excitement was growing in me. All at once I was running again. I ran around the block and past the coffee house. I ran up to Lincoln Park and sank down on the grass under the trees. My heart was pounding. I lay there looking at the moon and stars. A cold blue star winked below the moon. I closed my eyes against that star. Suddenly everything was spinning around me until it seemed by the awful beat of my heart that the earth itself had slipped from the hand of God and was falling in the night, unremembered.

16

Two days later we buried my father beside my mother in Calvary Cemetery. After the ceremony at the grave our neighbors followed us back to leave the death at H. C. Kowal's Funeral Parlor on Professor Avenue. Anna Kowal served butter cookies and coffee. I sat with Nina and Andy. As in the past two days it seemed we were sitting in freezing white light while everyone else lounged in the sun. The neighbors were making plans for the future. I thought of delicate glass bells that would break on ringing.

Finally the three of us went back to the house in Lincoln Court. Nina prepared lunch. She fried bacon and eggs. Sophie had baked a loaf of white bread as a gift for us. Nina toasted six slices of it. We ate in silence. It was right after the meal that Andy started to move nervously from room to room. He glanced at Nina in a significant way. She cleaned the table and then she went to lie down in my room. Andy sat across from me.

"Are you feeling all right?" he said.

"I guess so."

"Do you feel like talking things over?"

"What things?"

"Well, Paul, your father left a sort of a will."

"A will? How do you know?"

"I found it in his dresser."

"You mean you went through his things?"

"I was looking for the insurance policy, Paul. I didn't go through his things for any other reason."

"What about the will?"

"About a month ago he put the house in your name."

"Did he? A month ago?"

"It's about a month."

"It's when he put me out. I guess he thought I couldn't take care of myself at all."

"He said you can do what you please with it. And then he said he knows you'll do the right thing by Nina if you sell it."

"What do you think about it?"

"I'm an outsider, Paul. I'm the kind of brother-in-law who comes in handy to make funeral arrangements and things like that. The truth is the truth. What can I say?"

"Say what you think."

"Well, it depends on you. What are your plans? Are you planning to live here by yourself?"

"I don't know, Andy. I didn't make any plans today."

"There's nothing for me to say if you decide to live here."

"What if I don't care about it?"

"The best thing then is to sell the house."

"Sell it then."

"Don't misunderstand me. If you want to stay here, Paul, that's the end of this as far as I'm concerned. Selling it is something else again. It's better to do it right away."

I had this urge to reach over and tickle him.

"Do what?" I said, teasing.

"Sell the house. Next month it'll be worth less. It's hard to sell old houses in the winter. They look worse than they are."

"I know you'll do what you think is best for me."

"Try to understand, Paul. I'm in an awkward position here. If I talked about this next week or even a month from now you'd still think it was a shame for me to bring it up."

"It's a shame to bring this up, Andy."

"It's not what I want to do. Well, that's not exactly true. The money will help us all. Maybe we can start a business or something."

"Do what you please, Andy. It doesn't matter to me. With him gone it doesn't matter if this house just blows away. Even then it would be better to sell it first. Don't you think so?"

"I understand how you feel, Paul."

"Now what else is on your mind?"

"Well, Paul, everything in the house is yours. But you

understand Nina wants a few things. To remember the family."

"I thought so. I expected it. Do you know a couple of weeks ago I took some pictures of myself? I'll have them enlarged for you."

"It's no use talking if you're going to act like this."

"Nina can have whatever she wants. You know that."

"I was thinking we should take what we need and then sell the rest with the house. How about the refrigerator?"

They wanted the refrigerator.

"I'll tell you what," I said. "You can have everything and I'll just take the refrigerator."

"All right, Paul."

Carefully I stepped down on his shoe under the table.

"Wait then," I said. "I'll take everything and you can have the ax. I'll do it for you and Nina."

"What ax?"

"Don't you know about the ax? It's hidden down in the cellar. My father's father gave it to him when he left the old country. And his father gave it to him. It's what they call an heirloom, Andy."

"You're on my foot."

"I'm sorry."

"It's all right," he said, wearily.

I felt a sudden pity for him.

"Listen then," I said. "Don't pay any attention to me. Nina can have the refrigerator and anything else she wants. She can even have the new television set. But you'll have to finish the payments."

"It's really kind of you, Paul. I mean it. There's something else I'd like to say."

"Say it then."

"You won't believe this, Paul, but I liked your father. I know we never made things easier for him. But it started wrong between us. It was all our fault. I admit it. It was all our fault."

"No use talking about it. I was with him all the time and I couldn't do the one or two things he wanted me to do."

Andy scratched his head and glanced around the kitchen. He was losing interest in the conversation.

"That's the way people are," he said.

"What do you mean?"

"Well, they save their time and their money and themselves. And what are they saving for?"

"You mean we're like misers?" I said, stepping on his shoe.

"That's right. You're on my foot, Paul."

"I'm sorry."

"Maybe I'll lie down awhile," he said.

I went out on the porch. I sat in the chair and rocked. There was the chill of winter in the air. Dead leaves were blowing. Smoke and fire climbed on the gray sky. I rocked and rocked.

Late in the afternoon Sophie Nowak came across the street with a white package. Smiling, she tapped the package and walked past me into the house. In a moment there was excited talk from the kitchen. I went inside. Sophie had brought some homemade *kielbasa,* a garlic sausage. Nina was delighted. Andy said the sausage would be good with beans and horseradish. He offered to go out and buy a jar of horseradish. Sophie said beet horseradish would be best of all with the sausage. Andy went out to buy a jar of beet horseradish.

"Is there anything I can do?" I said.

"Nothing," said Sophie. "Just wait."

I turned away from Sophie. Something was coming loose inside me. I turned to Nina and waited.

"How are you feeling, Paul?" she said, finally.

"Well, Nina, I'll tell you how it is. Ten minutes ago I didn't think we had a chance. Any of us. I mean it. Now everything looks a little different. Maybe this sausage will be a turning point."

"What's the matter with you?" she said.

"I feel a little strange. I really do. I was sitting on the porch there and I was thinking about Pa. Do you know what I used to say to him sometimes? I used to say, 'Well, sir, we meet again.' I had this feeling he liked to hear crazy things like that. Guess what? I forgot what happened. I was rocking there on the porch and I was expecting him to come out any minute. Do you know what? The first thing I was going to say was, 'Well, sir, we meet again.' "

Every weekend during that autumn I went out to Calvary Cemetery. The neighbors heard about it. They gave me money to buy flowers for the graves of their loved ones. The cemetery was divided into sections and the sections were divided into ranges of graves. I walked up and down those curving green lanes. Laden with flowers, I spent whole afternoons looking for the graves of strangers. I would save my father and mother for last. Once it was dark by the time I found the son of Rakowski and I went home without stopping at the grave of my father. It came as a shock to find in that cemetery another mother and father and son and daughter and sister and brother. It seemed that everybody was there. Even more bewildering was the fact that my neighbors went on working and laughing and making plans as though nothing had ever happened. I would go looking for them.

"I found your son's grave," I told Rakowski.

"Thank you, Paul, thank you. Did you buy that pot with the nails in the bottom? Did you put the flowers in?"

"Yes, I did."

"How does that stone look to you?"

"The boy was sixteen years old when he died."

"That's right, Paul. Stanley was sixteen."

"Wasn't he your only son?"

"That's right. There's only the girl left. Let's go up and I'll buy you a beer at the Dew Drop. How about it?"

"I don't want a beer. You ought to be ashamed of yourself."

"I'm sorry, Paul. You're still feeling bad, eh? Wait a minute. I meant to tell you about Boganowski."

"Boganowski?"

"Henry Boganowski. Henry used to work with me in the mills. He used to operate the whirly crane. The man never married and he didn't have a relative here. I took care of his funeral. But now I can't remember where he's buried. I think it's near the railroad tracks. I was looking for him a couple of times and I couldn't find him. Let me know if you run across him."

"What if I do?"

"Let me know where he is," said Rakowski. "And put a flower on his grave while you're up there."

"Why don't you go up and put your own flowers? Why should I put flowers on his grave? I didn't even know him."

"Your father did. Henry was a good man in his way. He deserves a flower, Paul."

"I'm sure he deserves a flower. They all deserve flowers. Flowers should rain from the sky on them day and night. It's about time you people woke up and realized what's happening here."

"Come up to the Dew Drop. I'll buy you a fish fry and we'll have a glass of beer. It'll take your mind off things."

"I don't want my mind off things!"

"All right then, Paul. Stop at the house for supper some night."

He squeezed my arm and walked away. I watched him go toward the Dew Drop. Surely he was dreaming. A moment later I thought that I was dreaming. In the end I thought that God was dreaming.

After returning from the cemetery on the next afternoon I went for a walk through the neighborhood. I stood on Clark Bridge for a while and looked down at the steel mills. Perched on the bank of the winding river were the fast-plant cranes. An ore boat was being unloaded. Hot puffs of white smoke went up from two of three cranes. Their buckets came up full from the boat and then swung to the end of the wings where they dropped the ore into the pit beyond a reddened concrete wall. High above was the black bridge crane that took ore from the pit into the mills. Smoke was everywhere on the gray sky.

I walked back to Lincoln Park. I thought of Peggy. It seemed years and years ago that we strolled and kissed there in the dark under the trees. Now there were dead leaves and empty wine bottles and a litter of newspapers on the grass. It started to rain. I stood under a tree. Rain came down harder. I went over to the coffee house.

I sat down and pretended to watch a card game. No one spoke to me. I was grateful. After a while Theodore beckoned. I got up and went over to him. He reached under the counter and handed me a bright new harmonica. It was twice as big as my own. I was afraid to look at Theodore. When I did he was looking over my shoulder at the gamblers.

"I picked that up for you," he said.

I said nothing.

"The man told me it's a Hohner," he said. "It's what they call a chromatic. Made in Germany. See that button? You press it and it plays a half a note higher. I don't remember everything he said. But he said it plays the sharps and flats, too."

"I don't know anything about it."

"I thought so."

"Besides, I don't play any more."

"I don't blame you. Do you want some coffee?"

I shook my head.

"I know how it is, Paul. I guess your father would know, too. He must've took it bad when your mother passed away."

He was looking over my shoulder.

"I was going through the Euclid Arcade," he said. "I saw that harmonica in the window. I thought of you. And then I was thinking maybe you'd want to make a song for your father. That's one reason I bought it. It was on sale, too."

I turned away.

Blindly I went out of the coffee house. Marko was laughing in the corner. His laughter followed me into the rainy night. I wanted to run away and hide and yet there was no place for me. I stepped into the doorway next to the coffee house. I sank down on the stone step.

Marko came out. His coat was thrown capelike over his shoulders. He was smiling and nodding and then he saw me. One look was enough to start him laughing again. Now he was pointing to that big harmonica in my hand. He cupped his hands around his mouth. He was pretending to play a harmonica. He shuffled around to the forlorn sounds he was making in the night. All at once his hands fell to his sides and his head went back in wild laughter. He moved away.

When Sophie Nowak found me in that doorway I was wet to the skin. She was carrying a cane umbrella. She leaned over and took hold of my arm. She shook me hard.

"Paul," she said, sharply. "Get up, Paul."

I stood up for her. She forced her arm through mine. We started to walk. She was trying to keep me under the umbrella. We walked close alongside each other. My steps were a little too long for her. We were bumping at the hips. I shortened my stride to be in rhythm with her. Presently we were marching as one in the night. The precise step of it seemed very jaunty to me. There was no place to go and so I found myself hoping that we would go on marching and marching.

Sophie took me to her house. She sat me down and wiped my hair and face with a towel. She took off my shoes and led me into a bedroom. She helped me out of my shirt and trousers and underclothes. I sat on the bed while she took off my socks. All I had left was the harmonica.

"Get right in bed," she said. "I had it ready. I was going to tell you to spend a few days with me. It will do you good. See how clean the bed is? The sheets dried yesterday in the sun. Don't they smell fresh? Give me the harmonica. I'll put it on the table here. . . . Never mind then, Paul. I'll be in the kitchen if you want me."

She kissed me on the mouth.

I turned my face to the wall. Rain drummed on roof and windows. Somewhere there was fire in the dark. I thought of my father lying in the wet black earth of that cemetery. Last of all I knew that I must make a song for him. And for my mother and my brother.

And for everyone else, too.